TALL TALES FOR DARK NIGHTS

Owen Elgie

*Octavia!
Always lock the doors!*

Copyright © 2016 Owen Elgie

All rights reserved, including the right to reproduce this book, or portions thereof in any form. No part of this text may be reproduced, transmitted, downloaded, decompiled, reverse engineered, or stored, in any form or introduced into any information storage and retrieval system, in any form or by any means, whether electronic or mechanical without the express written permission of the author.

This is a work of fiction. Names and characters are the product of the author's imagination and any resemblance to actual persons, living or dead, is entirely coincidental.

The views expressed in this work are solely those of the author and do not necessarily reflect the views of the publisher, and the publisher hereby disclaims any responsibility for them.

ISBN: 978-1-326-82076-3

PublishNation
www.publishnation.co.uk

*For those who helped and those
who were always there for me.*

Also by this Author

The Circle of Fire
The Circle of Duty

Forced New Life

We've been separated for so long.

Thinking back, I never really appreciated the family that I had growing up. From the time that I was the smallest I can remember, I was always surrounded by such a close group that it left me nothing to be worried about. There was always conversation and a feeling of the truest togetherness.

We lived in a small community on an idyllic island. The days were warm and the nights cool. There were so many of us who grew up together. We all used to hang out together and the life we led was relaxed and fulfilling. They really were a good bunch.

That was then.

As I sit here, I think back to the life I had and wonder what has become of all of those that I remember. I'm alone now. Not isolated as one but plucked from that group. I'm now surrounded by strangers from other lands who are so far removed from me as to be utterly alien. Different colours are everywhere.

But we do share a horrible bond.

We were all wrenched from our homes, pulled from the lands that we knew and transported far away. The stories that are told, I can't understand them all, seem to be saying the same thing. All of us were crammed into different tight transports and hurried away from the ones we love.

We all found ourselves being hustled and split apart as we were bought and sold by different groups. Coins were changing hands right up to the end where I was placed with these others. You can see the harshness of the transport on the skin of the unlucky ones. They are all covered in ever darkening bruises.

It's cold here.

We all now sit staring from our wooded prison waiting for our end to come. I can feel myself and those others around me all withering away as the time we spend stripped from our roots passes.

What will be the end for me?

Looking around where I am I can see such comfort but I can see that I'm here only for the short term.

I really miss my family.

It's tough being a banana.

Funny Men

When you leave the house with your friends as a child, you're told to always be careful. You're told to not be out too late. And you're told not to talk to strangers.

It's good advice.

Not that all strangers are out to do the unthinkable to young children. The vast majority of people you don't know as a child are like you and I. If we saw a child in distress, we would help them to resolve whatever the problem may be.

But every parent has the fear that one of the relative hand full of bad apples in the population will be the one to cross paths with their precious off-spring, hence the warning to avoid contact with anyone they don't know.

As I said, it's good advice.

But,

There are some reasons which are much more powerful than the simple concern of stranger danger.

You can't always see this danger, but it can be anywhere at any time. The hidden threat can almost be heard on the wind when they approach, out on the edges of your awareness. The largest number of the population couldn't even register their arrival in a town but there will always be those, mainly children but not always, who are sensitive in the right way to register that there is something so very wrong and it's drawing closer.

Reports of sightings at the times of this creeping fear that is breathed in by everyone have given sketchy reports of someone being near that, somehow, is able to get close to children despite its true absolute horror. Well dressed in suits or uniform. Tales have been told of a pale, chalk white face with distorted features sitting atop a body which has been described as being like wire, like a child stretched to beyond adult height or like a moving skeletal frame.

But it's strong. So strong that if its long finger wraps itself around your arm, there will never be a way to unfurl it.

The stories are more akin to whispers from history than statements from anyone real. Everyone will have heard the story from someone who heard it from someone and so on.

So, to all the parents, hell, to everyone who has children in their family or community, the next time your child and their friends rush out to play at the local park or in any other location, just stop to think. Has there been any examples of anyone you or your friends know finding it impossible to sleep? Have there been people complaining of an unseen and powerful dread creeping over them? Have these people experienced this before? Long ago when there was a rash of child abductions?

Don't let the kids go out.

Lock the doors and windows.

Draw your loved ones to you and beg the fates that you are spared.

Look around your street. At the end of the road. On top of the nearest hill. Just beyond the edge of the local wood. There may be nothing to see but there may be, just maybe, a fleeting glimpse of a long spindly limb moving as if nudged by the wind. There could be that mask-covered face beaming out its twisted rictus.

Out at the edges of awareness but threatening every day to push in just a little further, will be something that is as old as time but so much more angry.

That presence which feels to be more in the mind but is reaching out an arm.

There are many.

The well-dressed, but utterly merciless,

Funny Men.

True Love

Chris ran a slow tongue over pristine teeth as Ashley's chest heaved.

The anticipation for both of them was building to such a level, they could both feel the impending crescendo.

Neither of them had experienced this before.

Chris lay on top of Ashley, making escape impossible.

"I do hope I haven't bound you too tightly my sweet Ashley."

Chris's voice showed the casual power being held over Ashley and it was clear that Chris was aroused by that power.

So new and so very intoxicating.

Ashley couldn't speak because of the satin scarf pulled tightly and knotted roughly.

All Ashley could do was emit a whimper.

And that was all Chris wanted.

To see Ashley waiting for whatever actions were about to unfold but with no power at all to stop them.

Chris knew which of them was really in charge.

"Are you ready Ashley?" Chris's face was all Ashley could see. It was so close they were almost touching noses.

Ashley knew not to move. Chris had made it abundantly clear what was expected in this exchange.

There wouldn't be any movement at all.

"Are you ready Ashley? I want to get started. I can't wait to explore you."

Their naked bodies writhed and squirmed on the red silk sheets as both accepted that the build up to this was about to spill over into action.

Moving bodily towards Ashley's face, Chris brandished a rigid six inches so close that the tiny breeze which came with the movement wafted Ashley's eyelashes.

The movement ended with Chris's tip resting on Ashley's chin, a gentle weight showing the crushing control.

A single tear rolled down Ashley's cheek.

Chris smiled, bearing the full wall of starkly white teeth.

"Oh come on baby. The wait's over now. I'm going to slip this inside you so hard. You really should just relax and let it happen."

Ashley gave up trying to keep the peace between them.

Gentle whimpering gave way to muffled screaming. The stillness was replaced by panicked bucking.

It lasted for hours for Ashley, the struggle. For Chris, just seconds.

But that was too long.

Chris couldn't wait for the fun to begin any longer.

With a swift thrust, all six inches slid inside and Ashley cried out against the satin scarf, screaming at the pain, at the force of what was happening.

It made no difference.

In, out, in, out.

Time and again Chris drove deep into Ashley and steadily the screams ebbed to barely a gargle behind the scarf.

Chris recognized that Ashley had utterly succumbed now and decided to make the most of the subservience.

"That wasn't that bad was it?"

Gasp from behind the scarf.

"Let's take this scarf off so you can tell me how much you love me."

Easing out of Ashley, Chris pulled the makeshift gag from place and allowed Ashley to speak.

"Well. Say something" Chris demanded.

Ashley's head fell to one side.

"Chris, what have you done?"

Silence.

Chris wiped blood from the knife that had just been used to full effect as the last piece of life left from Ashley.

Chris felt drunk on the power and knew that this most intoxicatingly, hypnotically compelling event must, just must, happen again.

Two Men Go Into a Bar

I watched the man leave the bar and venture into the liquid black of the surrounding night. The time had passed from nimble evening into resolute night as we had spoken of life, love and all things which fill the spaces in between. The end destination of our verbal travels makes me shudder to comprehend what it could mean.

I had been spending a short free time between the labours of the day and the relaxation of the evening within the welcoming embrace of a hard earned drink. Just a jot to ease the unwinding from the stresses of the day.

As I sat at the bar, watching other patrons come and go, I found myself joined by another who carried the air of someone wanting to relax and be rid of the day just encountered. For a long minute we both sat, staring ahead while looking at nothing – all the time enfolding our similar drinks in our left hands. He was a man of advancing years with a great many years experience showing in his grey hair. He was wearing a suit of similarly advanced vintage and, as I had noted before, he carried the air of one looking to rid himself of the day just passed.

It was this stranger who spoke the first words between us.

"I don't know about you but my day today has been chaotic to say the very least."

His voice was a deep, welcoming thing which made me just know that he had been directing his comment to me. There wasn't anyone immediately near to either of us save for the other but it took me a heartbeat to register the commencement of conversation and my response bore all of the hallmarks of one who had been caught off guard by the questioning of another.

"That bad eh?"

The stranger slowly sipped his drink as he considered my, oh so erudite response, still staring straight ahead.

"It's been so busy I just don't have enough time to do anything I want to get done. You know?"

That next sentence did make more sense to me as I had been prepared for the query but I truly did know. I had spent the days of my waking endeavour fighting against the unending passage of the sands of time. I nodded my agreement with my companion, taking a drink of my own as I did.

"There's never enough time is there?" He spoke again, reinforcing his point and drawing me fully into the conversation, taking another sip as he finished his speech.

"But we've all got our jobs to do regardless of us," he continued. "I don't know about you but my company expects more and more but heaven help anyone who can't deliver."

He took another drink as I absorbed what he had said.

"Keep on working hard and the rewards will come, though," was all I could think of saying in response. It seemed to me to show an understanding of his plight but showed that I had my own feelings on the pitfalls of hard work.

My companion nodded to himself at my comment, still staring straight ahead but now he carried the mantle and visage of one who was filled with regret. He spoke again.

"That's the challenge we all have though, isn't it? We all have to maintain a firm sight of what it is we place true value on. My working life has taken me to far off lands, allowing me to see and learn a great many things, but it's only now that I've come to the hollow understanding of my greatest mistake."

I could see that he was under a great stress or weight and that he was feeling a palpable futility of a lifetime of labours to either an uncaring or unforgiving master. I knew myself, the sensation of long hours worked and the expectations of delivering ever more but I still carried the energy and enthusiasm of youth. My companion, though, was jaded by the passing of long years. I could see stretched out before me the open fields of possibilities, of success and reward yet to come and those lush lands held promises of both personal and professional resolution.

My companion remained looking directly ahead but snorted out a dismissive laugh. I sat looking sideways at him as we both took another drink.

"The future is a wonderful place to gaze upon, I know, but like so many destinations, it will seldom be as it had appeared during the journey."

How had he been able to decipher so perfectly what my mind had been saying? How had he been able to pull from my head those thoughts that I had refrained from giving to speech?

He spoke again before I was able to utter any further sound, his forward focused gaze now both filled with the distant sadness and with a new determination of purpose.

"I was like you once. I expected to reap tomorrow the rewards of what I had sown today, but understand, tomorrow will never arrive for you. Just as I have done all of my life, you will work harder, give more effort and time until you realise too late that the future you have travelled towards is nothing but an obelisk to the ruined memories and hopes you once held so dear. You will be left to beat your bleeding hands against it as you curse its being. Your current destination is nothing more than a mirage you've created to justify what you are doing now."

He still remained transfixed ahead, speaking to me without regarding me in any way. What had started as being a conversation between two men winding down the day was developing into the opening salvos of a verbal battle – insults and recriminations flying wildly. I now turned to face him fully in preparation of my retort to him.

"The future will only be the wasteland of regret if you let it be. I know that my hard work now will bear fruit for me as time passes and my working life will be all the better for what I do now."

He considered this for half a second before replying, still looking ahead.

"Your *working life*. What about the remaining parts of your life? Don't you want to find love?"

"Love can't be planned but if it is waiting for me in the future then I will find it. You can't make the affections of others do your bidding can you?"

"But how do you know love is waiting for you in the future? You have to be available for it. If all you have is work then you'll never allow yourself to be in a position to meet the one person in the world who will be the completing piece of the puzzle of your life."

It was at that moment that my companion finally turned to face me. We sat eye to eye in an anonymous bar in the bustling streets of the surrounding metropolis. From this new position, I could see that his eyes were of a sparkling blue that held the sadness and fire of earlier but now with much deeper force pushing behind all of his emotions. Looking across those eyes to the other features of the man made me fall to speechlessness. His features had been weathered by the on-going effects of age and experience but there was a thunderous familiarity to him.

It was then that he spoke his final words to me.

"Please listen to the cautions of an old man who has seen just these things come to be. When I was your age I strove hard to deliver more and more and to do it faster and with less, all the while believing that my rewards would be forthcoming after a time. Those rewards will never come to you as they never came to me.

You are in a position now to understand what value there is in the pursuit of your truest wants, not those of expectations. Believe me Magnus, you are destined to find yourself in my chair in the future should you continue on as you are and not alter the focus of your life."

With no further comment, he drained what had remained of his drink and rose from his seat. He headed steadily for the door but paused slightly before he walked through, casting his eye around in a final gesture of remembrance before he left.

I sat and stared at the door as it swung shut behind him. I had understood from his face that he had been speaking a terrible truth to me. I had understood when he had used my name, though I had never given it to him. I understood all of his pains and regrets were destined to become mine unless I did exactly as he had explained and withdrew from the rat race my life was becoming.

All of this I understood, completely and without hesitation, as I knew that for some unfathomable reason or method, on that night, both of us had been speaking to ourselves.

Book Shop

The high street in most towns is a very odd place to find yourself. It's becoming that almost every town has at its centre a clone of every other town centre. The same shops and services are wedged together and fighting for your attention. The large chains are the ones who've managed to squeeze themselves into the spaces on the roadways, puffing out their collective chests until all of the smaller companies, the family run local businesses, have been popped out like a teenager's acne.

Kerry walked down the road and let her attention wander. She knew exactly what was at each location along the road so didn't need to pay any attention to what was happening in the windows of the various retailers. The same offers of money off or '2 for 1' offers beamed out at her with rictus expressions from every window she passed by. She could swear that all the shops just handed the posters around each week so they all had a chance to proclaim the same deals. Aside from the other shoppers milling around, she could practically walk down the street blind folded and still be able to have a pretty good stab at naming the deals in all of the shops.

The only points of individuality she could see in her town were now right out at the very edges of the shopping experience. The back alleys and hidden nooks held the only independent locations to buy anything but even they were feeling the pinch. A scented candle shop sat on the first floor above a café. The café had previously been Jones and Daughters but was now part of a national chain. The advertising hording for the café was bold and brash and took all of the attention in the area. The small sign proclaiming the candle shop didn't stand a chance.

Kerry liked the candle shop. She'd liked the woman behind the counter who'd served her and she liked the constant smell of sweety goodness which hung around the place like an intoxicating cloud. She smiled to herself as she thought about the sheer enveloping loveliness of the associations which came to mind but that smile was quick to fade when she closed the gap to the shop in question. The small sign proclaiming its existence had been joined by a much larger sign, boldly stating that they were going out of business. Kerry sighed and walked on. Just too niche a business to survive I suppose. The café below was doing a roaring trade and had tables on the street outside all filled with people happily sipping on assorted hot beverages. Kerry thought about going in but didn't fancy the crush at the counter waiting to be served.

Rounding the next corner, she continued walking without paying any attention to the details of the buildings or the people around her. She missed the small personal touch. She pondered what the café owners had done to make such a success of their business when the previous owners had found it so difficult. All the backing from a massive national chain must be able to do so many things in terms of advertising and revenue generation. That said, maybe they were just better at business.

That was the last thought that crossed her mind regarding the potential prowess of local businesses as she was snapped back into the here and now by the beaming face of the young man with the flyer in his hand.

"Would you like to have a free coffee as you browse through our collections of some of the most wonderful books ever written? Our prices are very competitive and you could find any number of works to bring all kinds of knowledge into your life."

Kerry floundered in her mind for a long second as she fought to line up everything her assailant had said. He, in turn, looked back at her, his hand outstretched with the flyer, by way of further emphasis. The second dragged on even further and his expression started to crack, his previous enthusiasm starting to melt away to reveal worry just beneath its surface.

Kerry spoke first.

"I haven't really got the time I'm afraid. I'm heading to work at the moment." She wasn't but that was her stock answer when dealing with people handing out flyers, charity box rattlers and the ambulance chasing law firms who offer the no win, no fee deals. It was usually enough to have the person in her path turned around and off to hassle someone else but this time the obstacle remained.

His facial expression had turned from the ever so subtle leaking of worry to an almost dread panic at the refusal. He tried again.

"You could be able to find the most amazing gifts for yourself or for friends and family. The wonder and magic of the written word. And did I mention, free coffee." He nodded nervously as he smiled at her, practically pleading for her to listen.

Kerry didn't have time for this. She could feel the response climbing up her throat until she realized where she was.

Only now did she start to take in the details of the street she was stood on. Without her being aware of it, without her being aiming for it she had casually wandered in a daydream into a very close little road which was lined with oddly shaped buildings with wonky windows and doors. On either side of her was hunkered a collection of the odd shaped business' which weren't a part of the shining beacon of order the high streets of the country have become. Here was where the small local businesses had chosen to hide, to shy away from the judgmental gaze of the uber shops who had been collectively kicking sand in their faces.

Kerry's complaint never got as far as being uttered.

Instead she looked back at the young man who was still smiling in that delightful 'please take a flyer I've not had anyone take one and I've been here for hours' kind of way.

She smiled at him.

"Lead me on to the books."

As they moved off in the direction of a particularly nobbly looking building, Kerry was struck by the now boundless energy which was pouring from every aspect of her guide. He'd breathed the sigh of relief of a man who had finally made a sale after far too long trying and had been garbling protestations of the outstanding nature of where they were heading. As they arrived at the heavy looking wooden door he was practically leaping from foot to foot like an over excited schoolboy.

"You really will be glad that you've taken the time to come in. There are all manner of options and genres for you to choose from, all guaranteed to give you a wonderful time in both the choosing and the reading."

Kerry nodded politely. She felt it was sweet that this poor flyer distributor was so passionately invested in the subject of his flyers. Maybe he was family. Maybe he was the owner. It made her feel good that the feeling of ownership was still alive and well in the back streets of her town. The call to a time gone by which she could see was still holding on for all it was worth.

He pushed the door open easily despite its heavy appearance and stepped inside ahead of her, holding the door open from inside and gesturing gallantly for her to enter. She nodded slightly to him in acknowledgement and slowly crossed the threshold.

The door shut behind her without a sound and she was left, for a second or two, to take in all of the details of the book shop which was stacked upon itself all around her, straining at the seams of the building it was housed in as if it had been designed for a space much larger and was having to make do with something at least two sizes too small. The air was thick with the smell of a thousand million pen strokes, a trillion key strikes on the keyboard and billions of hopes, thoughts, dreams and ideals. The atmosphere held a comfortable warmth which comes from the tattered pair of slippers which have seen their best days pass them by, of the comfort blanket treasured by the adults remembered childhood or the smell of a loved one on a piece of clothing. Kerry could feel the tensions of life just draining away as she breathed in the coffee and adventure in the air. She had been in the larger bookshops which are in the larger towns, the book superstores, where almost every conceivable title or genre is held under the one roof, and felt utterly disconnected from everything there, but this place carried with it a subconscious lure towards the myriad pages which could be inside. This small business had managed to do something in a fraction of a heartbeat which the superstores had never been able to do. It made her want to explore the space and to hell with the consequences of cost.

Looking around her, she found that her young companion had left her. Looking through the glass panes of the door she could make him out on the roadway beyond, flyer in hand, checking his watch as he looked left and right, obviously checking for more passersby to entice towards the shop.

"So I'm on my own then." She whispered the words to herself and was about to head into the nearest corridor of bookshelves when she was answered.

"Not quite. What would you like to see?"

The voice came from everywhere yet from nowhere. It drifted out to her from almost behind yet ahead and to both sides of her. She looked around, hunting for the source of the sound amidst the stacked paper and shelving.

"I'd like to see fantasy fiction if I could." She was still looking around her but there was still no sign of her new accompaniment.

"Ahh. We have so many wonderful works in that area. You will really have the most wonderful time with us." The voice still wafted on the air like a delicate scent, teasing her with its nebulousness.

"Would you like some coffee before we start? It is free." She spun round sharply as the voice was finally solidified to a point behind her. She turned quickly, not sure what she was going to find, and was confronted by a tall, lean man of late middle age, holding a small coffee pot with steam curling from the spout in one hand and a small china cup in the other.

"I'm sorry my dear. Did I startle you? The acoustics in this old place do seem to play tricks no matter what I say to them." He smiled and his face creased at the edges. He was wearing the effects of time all over his face but it looked good on him.

"Don't panic. You sounded like you were miles away. No thank you for the coffee." Kerry re-gathered herself and felt more comfortable. He looked at her, still with the same casual smile playing across his features as he put the pot and cup down on a nearby table.

"We'll just get straight down to business then. Where would you like to go today? Which fantastical journey would you like to embark upon?"

"I like reading Jim Butcher novels. And Ben Aaronovich, Neil Gaiman and Terry Pratchett. What have you got of that sort?"

Kerry had always enjoyed books. The feeling of walking through a secret gateway to another world when you started reading was almost intoxicating. Even encyclopedias had a similar draw. They were the gateways to knowledge. Labyrinthine palaces holding facts and figures which had the power to astound and to terrify all at once. There was no way to know who you'd be after reading anything, such was the power of the written word.

"Hmmmm. They are very good authors indeed. Make me smile as well. What can I suggest that is likely to give you the best experience of your time with us?" The man regarded her as he spoke and considered the options open to him as he sagely rubbed at his chin. Finally he asked,

"When is your birthday?"

"Thirteenth of April," Kerry responded almost immediately. It could have been easy for her to be offended by the question or at the very least be a little put out by it, but she saw no malice at all behind the question. She could see that whatever the question was being asked for, it was going to add a vital ingredient to the broth of opportunity which was being concocted in his head.

The man considered her answer with more chin rubbing and the occasional nod.

"Then I have the perfect title for you my dear. I can give you a story which will give you enjoyment and that lovely warm feeling of reminiscence which won't end in the way you'd expect. Does that sound like the kind of story you'd be interested in?"

She looked at him and was hooked. He had been so expressive in the few words on the topic he had uttered that she couldn't stop herself from wanting to find this tale and burrow directly into it.

"That sounds wonderful. Who is it by? What's it called?"

"Don't worry about either of those trivial details. I would suggest that you just read the book without knowing either. You will read every word with such focus and attention that the story will come alive in your mind without any effort."

"But I'll be able to see the title if I buy it. I'm not going to keep my eyes closed all of the way home."

"I would suggest that you take the chance to read some of the work here before you decide if you want to buy it. If you have the time, we have a small reading nook at the back of the shop which you could use to try the book on for size. How does that sound?"

Kerry considered his words. She had been casually drifting through the town centre on a warm summer lunch time when she had been stopped. She wasn't expected anywhere today and she'd completed everything she'd planned to do in town. What was there to stop her relaxing into the first few chapters of this offered masterpiece?

"Sounds great. Take me to the book." She smiled at the man in the shop and he smiled back at her.

"This way please."

He led her through the aisle on the left of her as she looked at the shop, passing casually through the towers of literature which were draped over the furniture like the branches of hundreds of aged trees. She could feel the floor boards creaking and shifting under their weight at each footfall as the whole building seemed to sway and twitch like a forest of words. After much longer than she would have thought possible in such an out of the way shop, she was led to a clearing within the woods and found the nook.

There were seven worn leather chairs unevenly spaced around the area, each with a small side table of ornate carved wood. Her guide was standing next to a large chair at the back of the group, set up against the back wall of the shop, his arm out in gesture to show that this was the best place for her to base herself for the read.

"Have a seat here. This chair will give you just enough of everything you need to really immerse you into the story. I'll go and find the novel for you. Are you sure I can't tempt you with a coffee?"

Kerry put her bag down next to the chair and settled into the soft leather.

"No thank you. I'll just have a read if I may."

He nodded slightly and turned sharply to head off down a different aisle than the one they had entered through. She turned her head away from his retreating form to take in the detail of the clearing she had been left in, but was startled when her companion re-appeared almost immediately.

"And here we are."

He lent forwards and presented her with a large, leather bound tome with no lettering of any kind on the cover. There was no indication what the book was called or who had written it.

"As I said, just read the words and feel their meaning. Pay no thought to who wrote it or what it's called. You will draw so much more from the reading this way."

With that he turned and headed back down the aisle they had originally walked down, calling over his shoulder as he went that if she needed anything just to call and he'd be with her immediately.

She noticed that the almost ethereal element to his voice was back and he sounded to her like he was walking back into a dream.

Finally she was alone with the book. This mighty story which had been sold so effectively to her that she was now on the verge of spending the whole afternoon in its company.

Opening to the first page, there was no introduction or acknowledgements or even chapter headings, the narrative just began.

April is a wonderful time to have a child. The weather is warm enough that you don't feel like you're in the merciless grip of winter but the rain will keep the world cool enough that any new arrival will be as comfortable as possible.

That was why he'd asked her date of birth. This was going to be one of those stories which had been tailored to the reader.

Kerry was a calm yet serious baby, in as much as any baby could be described as being serious, but she gave both Jeff and Victoria such a feeling of contentment and wholeness that they could scarcely remember a time when they hadn't been her parents.

Kerry was surprised with the level of detail which was included in the early part of the novel. All the details of her family were correct and she could remember them describing her as being serious throughout her life. She'd always thought that the description of serious was very vague and her parents had been oddly unable to give any further explanation when she'd pushed them. Who knows, maybe whatever it was she had done as a child which had caused the name would be in the pages before her.

She carried on with a small smile on her face.

As page after page was turned, sentence after sentence was devoured with the eyes of purest fascination, the narrative became one of the mundane yet vital facts that are existence for each and every one of us. There were tales of the life of a protagonist who grew up in a supportive household and all of the tiny adventures she had embarked upon over the course of her life. There was a collection of tales recounting the firsts of any child's life, step, word, day at school, broken bone, boyfriend, driving lesson and car. The competing melodies of tales of parent's woes and wonders, sibling's adventures and of familial deaths all layered themselves into the symphony that was the life of our heroine. They would occasionally threaten to overpower everything that was happening but in each and every case or event, our protagonist, Kerry, was able to push through to reach a conclusion which would give her some kind of lesson.

Kerry read through the instances of her own life from the detached viewpoint of the reader. She remembered incident after incident as she relived them all in an effortless detail, as if the greatest purveyor of the written word had been following her around for the whole of her life, recording the details for this very moment.

It made her feel simultaneously nostalgic and unnerved. Who'd put this together?

"Excuse me," she called out, placing the book down on the side table and waited for a response.

"Can I get you anything?" came the nebulous voice. "Coffee?"

"I'd like to speak with you please. I have a question about the book."

"Of course." His tone was one of spider silk and whispers, coming from a point beyond her field of vision.

And then he was next to her, standing casually to attention like a butler would in so many stories which have been told before.

Kerry jumped slightly but not enough to break her stride.

"Where did this book come from? I thought that it was one of those stories which was created to include the reader in the story very literally but you couldn't have just had this available for everyone, ready to dig out when you find out their birthday. How have you been able to truly have the story of my life in this shop?" Kerry had managed to keep her tone as close to matter of fact as she could but there was no mistaking the undertone of worried enquiry which it was trying to hide.

The man just looked at her with a neutral expression on his face.

"Doesn't this story give you a feeling of familiarity? Don't you feel a level of engagement with the characters that you haven't felt in a book before?"

Kerry felt ill at ease as he just stared at her. He must have noticed.

"I know this feels a little odd but there isn't a catch at all. This is truly a work which has been created to entertain and enthrall. After all, there are only so many stories to be told, that's why they have the disclaimers on things like this, 'Any similarity to people living or dead' and all that." He smiled effortlessly and she could feel the tension ease a little.

"Here, have a cup of coffee as you read. By the looks of things there is still a fair way for you to go." A cup of steaming coffee had suddenly appeared on the arm of the chair she was sat on. The man smiled and turned away. In seconds he was gone down a different aisle.

She considered his words and tried to think of a way anyone could have had events line up so perfectly that they would have all of the details of her life available to put in a novel and know that she would be here, in this shop, at this time when she hadn't known she was going to be here. Maybe there had been a fantastical alignment of details and she had just been given the one book which would make her think back over all of the details of her own life and see that she was the protagonist. Her parent's names weren't uncommon. Neither was hers. Surely everyone had had variations on the themes of the same experiences when they were growing up. That was why horoscopes worked so well, everyone could make the story fit themselves.

She sipped at the coffee and tried to make herself relax. This was a wonderful book for drawing the reader in. It looked like Kerry may have been pulled in just a little too much.

Putting the cup down on the table and retrieving the book, she remembered that she didn't really like coffee. Why had she drunk it?

Wow this book was making her mind race in some very strange directions. Resolving to maintain a greater level of control over her own psyche, she settled back and climbed back into the pages.

She rejoined the action with the heroine Kerry about to leave to go to university.

Jake had gone with them when the family had taken Kerry off to her new life at the University of Canterbury. He wanted to spend the maximum amount of time with his girlfriend as he could before she was living away from him. It had been an Indian summer that year with the temperatures in late September climbing to almost concerning levels. Indeed, there had been much talk of global warming and climate change during the journey.

Kerry could remember the journey they'd gone on in what was now terrifying detail. Her boyfriend at the time, Jake, had been with them when she had gone off to university. He'd been the one talking about the horrors of man-made climate change and her father had spent the entire journey grinding his teeth at the noise he was making. Kerry's father hadn't liked Jake. Jake had been Kerry's first real boyfriend so he was naturally akin to the devil in her father's eyes.

Kerry kept thinking that this was just a story. She was projecting her own life experience onto what was happening and she wasn't just reading her own life. She couldn't be.

She continued to push through the gluey familiarity of the tale on the pages. She could feel each and every detail dragging behind her like an anchor, each sentence adding more weight to her fears that there was something more at work than just a story.

The time she'd dyed all her clothes pink thanks to the rogue red sock in the whites wash. The time she'd just tried that new drink everyone was raving about and ended up spending three days perched over the toilet. The time she'd fallen in love with a complete stranger and dumped Jake. All these and all of the other memories were there. Her first job, first flat everything was there for whoever picked up this novel. It was much more than just being the similarity of stories, the shared thread of existence. She was truly reading page after page of her own life that was being recounted for the entertainment of anyone who could read.

She felt violated. Someone had stolen her life and claimed it as their own work. She couldn't stop reading despite the trepidation she felt. Until she reached the most terrible passage of the book.

She walked in a haze of her own thoughts and paid no attention to the details around her. She'd seen the effects of the new wave of business and the candle shop closing was going to grate on her for a very long time. She didn't know truly why but she knew that she had just lost a very important piece of her understanding of the world. It was at that moment that the young man with the flyer jumped out in front of her.

She threw the book away from her and it landed at the feet of the shop keeper.

"W-w-w-w-what is this? Who are you?" Her voice was trembling and cracking as she fought to express the sheer brutality of what she'd just gone through. The man just stood and stared at her, still with the same expression of caring detachment. Reaching down, he retrieved the book and closed it, being careful not to crease any of the pages.

"Who I am doesn't matter. All you need to concern yourself with is the rest of this book." He cradled the volume to his chest and stared at her.

Kerry said nothing. What could she have said? What could she have possibly said that would have fit into the space left by his words. He noticed the turmoil in her.

"Let me explain." He settled himself down into a chair next to her and placed the book purposefully down on the table next to her.

"You know that this is the story of you, don't you?"

She nodded quickly, her eyes wide and not leaving his.

"You've been brought here to give you a choice." He gestured at the whole space around him, showing that the shop was more than just a business. "This is the book of your life but as you can see it includes everything." He lifted the pages up slowly and let them flick through his fingers, showing Kerry that there was print on every page, including beyond the point she had reached.

"This is the story of all of your life, from beginning to end. The choice I give to you is this. Knowing that you can read all of the details of your life to come, will you continue to read to the final page?"

"How is that possible? How can you see the future?" She'd been convinced that the story was her but the future was another thing all together.

The man slowly pulled out his pocket watch, a battered yet ornately designed piece, and casually flicked the cover open. In the air above her was suddenly cast a huge clock face, very much like the face's on the Big Ben tower. Its massive hands stood like guarding weapons before the detail of the mechanism behind. Kerry just stared at it, her mouth open and her mind racing.

"I have an ability, in that field. What you can see here is time itself. I can see so much. I can see all of the colours and sounds of the ever flowing river which is time. I can also have an effect on the actions of the currents."

Reaching out a hand, he casually waved his long fingers and the hands of the clock before her started to move rapidly forwards, revolving many times faster than the normal passing of time. Kerry watched on as, from outside the shop, the sun began to set and rise rapidly, in keeping with the movement of the hands of the clock. Kerry watched as first days, then months, rushed past at the behest of the mysterious shop keeper.

"How are you doing that?" Kerry just couldn't understand.

"As I said, I have an, ability. Here, in this place, I sit beyond time, my island in the river, and I can bend the fabric of time to my will."

He flicked his hand the opposite way and the passage of time reversed, returning Kerry to her present.

"And here, you too are immune to the effects of time. Outside, everyone you know had just registered that you had been missing for years, yet you have not aged to match their appraisal of the situation."

"But what do you want with me?" Kerry was struggling to keep up with the fantastical story which was being spun for her but she needed to know what was going to happen to her. He closed the watch and the image of the giant swirling vortex of time blinked out.

"I'm here to give you the chance to read the book of your life. I want you to decide now if you're prepared to know what will happen to you next. Do you want to see if you die tomorrow in a terrible accident? Do you have a long drawn out illness which claims your life? Do you win the lottery? I want you to weigh the facts and decide if you want to know the future."

She just couldn't believe him.

He had to be lying.

But what if he wasn't?

"If I read it all and discover something bad, I could just avoid the situation couldn't I? Just sidestep your book."

"You could indeed. But, all of our lives are examples of choices which lead to others. You could avoid the death sentence tomorrow but that could lead to creating a different one the day after. One, I might add, you would then be blissfully unaware of."

"Then what's the point of knowing anything if you will only make one change before the knowledge is then obsolete? I choose to go now." She felt belligerently confident at the application of her logic at showing this man that he wasn't going to scare her. He considered her words carefully, again with the same sage chin stroke he had used before.

"But what if that one action is all you have to avoid? What would happen if not getting onto the plane you know is going to crash opens up the life that could have been. Wealth, fame, happiness could all be there if only you hadn't died." He sat there, still with his hand on his face, and watched her think.

What if? There could be so many possibilities?

"Why would you give me the chance to know? Why pick me?"

"I can see everything that is, was and will be. I know all that is knowable in the universe but I find myself to be in need of interaction with those who exist in the flow of time. I can see that you are all vulnerable and I find that is a trait I lack. I have no natural predators. Not even age will have any kind of effect on me. I like you and enjoy spending time with you, if you'd excuse the pun."

"The lad outside. That was you, wasn't it." Kerry felt that she was starting to become acclimatized to the conversation so thought she would try asking for some more detail.

"Oh no, his name is James. He's been with me for some time."

That wasn't what she had expected to hear and it did knock her over slightly. She felt like a novice ice skater who had been feeling that they were getting somewhere when they suddenly ended up on the backside on the hard cold surface. She just couldn't hold onto what was being said.

She needed to be out of this situation.

"I chose to leave the book here thank you." Decisive action. She was reasonably sure that she had chosen the right direction but there was always the chance that she was going to be passing over the greatest gift anyone was ever offered.

"Are you sure Kerry? You could be handing back the key to the most wonderful life. Are you certain that you are making the right decision?" There was still no kind of pleading to his voice, just the same casual tone as he maintained his neutral expression.

"I'm sure. The fun comes from not knowing. Surely that's why you do this in the first place. You don't have any fun because you know everything that's going to happen. This whole situation is you having fun." Kerry finally knew she'd worked out everything and knew that she wasn't going to be the unwitting puppet in the actions of someone claiming they were the controller of time.

"That was why you were pushing the coffee all of the time. You knew that I hated coffee but you wanted to push me around to accept it. That was just a game to you, wasn't it?"

There was no further conversation on the point but he had a faintly content expression on his face.

He stood and picked the book up, smiled at her, and gestured for her to follow him back to the front of the shop. She did and felt a wonderful warmth as she considered a new found positivity of the journey ahead of her in life. She could feel the possibilities of the years opening up ahead of her and knew that she would encounter every problem which presented itself and overcome them all. She knew she'd made the right choice.

"I thank you greatly for your time with me. You have truly given me a wonderful experience." He bowed ever so slightly and opened the door for her. The cool air of late afternoon drifted into the shop and wafted through Kerry's hair.

She stepped through the door and onto the footpath beyond.

James was nowhere to be seen. He'd obviously finished his stint trying to attract business, or was it interest he was attracting?

Kerry took in a deep breath of air and looked forward to the mystery of the time to come, knowing that even one detail of the future could have awful effects on the life of anyone. She would just have to make do with having fun with the not knowing. Turning back to the shop she discovered with a shock that there was just a wall of old brick behind her. The shop, with all of the tomes of who knows whose lives, was gone and the proprietor had gone with it. Maybe he'd wound his clock on to find a new person to play with?

Smiling to herself, she stepped off the pavement.

But didn't see the car.

The Power of Love

The car crunched along the damp gravel driveway towards the house, more akin to a furtive burglar than anything heralding the arrival of honest guests. Every pop and crack from the tiny stones under the weight of the tyres felt as if it was being greeted by accusing stares and frowns of disgust from the surrounding landscape, *how dare it break the silence we've been working so hard to build?*

Mark edged the car forwards up the drive anyway. He and Sara had been travelling for hours and they would have to just put up with the perceived stares from the bushes and outbuildings. He still didn't go too fast though, just in case.

They'd been on the road for most of the day, fighting against both the elements and the population. The first part of the journey had been out of the city so they'd been caught in jam after jam as they fought their way through the transport arteries of a city which looked like it had been living on an awful diet. Sara had counted up that there had been a total of four clear roads on the journey from their home and through the metropolis, totaling about half a mile of actual travelled distance. The fatty blockages of road works were doing their best to bring on the gridlock heart attack they always threatened and no-one seemed to care.

After three hours of frustration under the grey cloudy sky of February, they finally made their way onto the motorway and the traffic began to move more freely. Maybe the roads outside of the city were just fitter?

"Finally we can get moving," sighed Sara from the passenger seat. Mark nodded his agreement as he pushed the speed up towards seventy. He would have continued the conversation longer but Sara had already dropped the seat back and was bedding down ready to sleep.

"Sleep well darling. I'll wake you up if anything exciting happens."

As expected, nothing exciting had happened. At all. Fields and rivers and forests and towns all whizzed past as the car ate up the miles.

After three more hours, the motorway gave way to smaller roads as they neared their destination. Mark had intended to leave Sara asleep all the way there but as the roads had got smaller, the bends in them had grown larger, the power in the relationship between the roads and the land shifting so it was easy to see which was boss. Those bends had been the reason she'd woken up, the constant change of inertia as the car swung round and she was forced awake.

"We almost there?"

"Pretty close. As long as we can stay on the road and not end up at the bottom of the valley we're driving along." Marks face carried the concentration clearly and, looking out, Sara could see why. The cloudy sky they had been driving under in the city had been replaced by rain and a howling wind. She could feel the car being tugged back and forth by it.

"Just be careful. This is our *honeymoon* you know." She spoke with a smile and rubbed his arm. They'd been married for years and honeymooned in India. This honeymoon had been booked almost before they had had a chance to decide if it was a good idea.

Like so many people these days, they both belonged to a discount club website. Every day they would receive an e-mail with the latest special offers and money off codes. More often than not they just deleted them without even bothering to read through what was there but for some odd reason, as coincidence so often seems to strike, they had both read this one. It had offered a long weekend stay in Anngross House, all inclusive at a rustic five star retreat set within miles of rolling countryside, utterly secluded from the stresses and tribulations of the outside world. It had been advertised at an eighty five percent discount which had been akin to one of those magical blue lights to flies and other bugs. They'd both clicked on the offer before they'd even bothered to read through the fine print of the deal. It was only open to newlyweds. And only those who were married within the last month.

They had both reasoned that as they hadn't asked for any kind of proof to be entered into the e-mail, that they couldn't have been that serious about the importance of the dates of their wedding. They had both been less certain when the e-mail arrived from the hotel explaining that they had been forced to cancel one couples booking as it had been discovered that they weren't even married but no such communication had landed with them. At least, they concluded, they were married.

And here they were.

After the weeks of worrying that they were going to be turned away (they'd even checked out other local inns and hotels just in case) and panicking that they were about to get into so much trouble, their inner teenagers coming out easily, they were finally sat in the rain soaked driveway at the maw of the hotel of potential judgement. The rain had at least stopped hammering down but the wind was still jouncing the car about even though they were stationary.

Looking out at the surroundings they could feel the accusing glares of each and every object, plant and brick of the hotel, all showing their utmost contempt. The car bounced and they looked on scared, feeling worse by the stately calm of the grounds.

Despite the stormy weather, all of the trees and bushes which had run alongside the driveway were serenely still. The pummeling fist of the wind which was smashing against the car was having no effect on the location itself. Could nature itself see through the charade they were about to perpetrate?

"Come on then. We can't just sit in the car." Mark was tired from the drive so needed to get settled, his own fears being over-ridden by the fact he'd been doing the driving.

Not another word was spoken. They both just climbed out of the car, fighting constantly against the continuously howling wind, and hurried into the hotel.

Through the heavy wooden doors they were greeted by a room which was equal parts Downton Abbey and Woman in Black. There were fixtures and fittings which leant suggestion to a very sedate country house but they were undercut by the amateur taxidermy hanging at numerous locations and the myriad paintings which contained stern faces and, in the background, nameless and faceless shapes brooding over the whole image. Very romantic.

The carpeting, paintwork and wallpaper were all worn just the wrong side of showing comfortable use. There were several patches throughout the area they could survey that were seemingly crying out for the care and attention of some loving DIY. Everywhere carried a perfect framing of a welcoming environment which wasn't as welcomed by those who it welcomed.

The reception desk ahead of them was set against the rear wall of the entrance hall and was decorated in every stereotype they could imagine. A large signing in book lay open and there was a large pen held by a chain affixed next to it. There was no computer that either of them could see, instead there were large binders proudly bearing the names of the months neatly arranged on a shelf at the back of the reception. February was open on the desk proper. There was even a small bell waiting to be 'dinged'.

Behind the desk, the massive staircase stretched up from right to left, climbing up to the high first floor. Looking up to the double height ceiling they could see another staircase climbing further back against the back wall of the building to a second floor, of which all they could see was the collection of dark wood balustrades which marked the edge of the elevated balcony.

The reception desk, though, was deserted.

"Looks a little creepy. You can see why they're offering an eighty five percent discount." Sara made her feelings very clear to Mark, but she still whispered just in case anyone else was about.

They both edged forward, taking in as much of the detail of their surroundings as they could, making their way towards the desk. The vestibule area remained devoid of human presence except for them as they crept forwards. Outside there was the continuing cacophony of wind rushing around the hotel as it had been as they arrived but there seemed to be only the noise of the wind itself to identify, rather than trees or other objects being affected. They must have been growing pretty hardy trees up here considering the fun and games Mark had experienced on the way here.

Arriving at the desk with still no sign of further company than the desk itself, the couple looked at each other for advice on the correct course of action.

"Looks like we should ring the bell." Sara looked up at her husband and it was clear that what she really meant was 'looks like you should ring the bell'.

Casting a final look around the room, Mark reached out and with as much force as he felt was proper, rang for all he was worth.

The chimes scuttled off through the hotel in different directions, each looking for anyone they could find to alert to the presence of others in the building. As the bell began to fall silent, they were again left with the wind outside as the only other noise. The air remained thick with both dust motes and a subtly perceived menace as the couple looked in all directions attempting to locate someone who could welcome them to the building. Still no sign of any kind of inhabitants.

Sara nudged Mark, making it painfully clear that she thought that he should be doing something to resolve this issue, although she was much less forthcoming with any kind of idea what it may have been. He was about to hit the bell again but this time more forcefully and with the added shout of 'hello' but his actions were halted as the previously unseen door which had been built into the rear wall of the reception area, began to inch its way, silently, open.

"I could have sworn that that was just a wall." Sara hadn't turned to speak directly to Mark as she watched on, not understanding how she had missed the door.

"Me too," Mark responded, similarly transfixed.

Mark and Sara remained motionless as the door made its painfully slow progress, revealing an ever expanding view of the blackness beyond. After a minute lasting a lifetime, the movement ceased and the previous cloak of stillness returned to the scene, the darkness which stood beyond the opening still taunting them with its promise of the unknown. The silence of the house gathered in around them and the pair could feel the increase in the tension they were feeling. Where were the staff? Where did the door come from? How did that door open?

The wind continued outside with the same ferocity and the couple stared into the darkness behind the reception desk without moving, the growing concern of the beyond petrifying them to rigid stillness. Without effort, every image of haunted houses swam through their minds and their skin began to buzz with perceived contact.

"Can I help you two?" squeaked from behind them.

They both jumped with the shock of the unexpected voice and Sara let out a startled yelp as the pair swung round to identify the source of the greeting.

In front of them stood a tiny woman of indeterminately old age. Her white grey hair was plastered down tight to her head and had been tied back to look as if it were under an enormous amount of tension. Her dress was very much in keeping with the estate as a whole, a long tweed skirt and plain white blouse topped with a dark red shawl gave her the perfect appearance of someone who was as at home within the estate as the other period pieces. She had a very welcoming face, if a little stressed, and, despite the shock she had given them, Mark and Sara were quick to feel comforted by her arrival.

"Hello," started Mark. "We have a booking for the weekend through one of those discount websites. Mr. and Mrs. Knight."

The woman frowned at him and just held his gaze. "Website?"

"The newlywed offer," interjected Sara, hoping that that would provide more of a jog to her memory.

The lady's face transformed into a relieved smile and she nodded enthusiastically.

"Certainly my dears, we've been expecting you. Didn't find the weather too bad getting here did you?"

"It's a little breezy out there isn't it? We almost got blown off our feet when we got out of the car." Sara struck up a conversation with their host as she walked between them and headed behind the reception desk.

She slowly eased the door closed and tutted as she did.

"Knows not to move but does so enjoy new faces."

Mark and Sara laughed nervously and just chalked it up to their hosts' eccentricity. She busied herself behind the desk but had a wide, thin smile on her face.

"So newly Mr. and Mrs. You must be so in love. I remember what that feels like; even if it has been a little while since my George and I married, rest his soul."

"I'm sorry for your loss." Sara liked the lady and gave both her and Mark's apologies.

The lady shushed her away and carried on regardless, still with the same smile on her face.

"We've got the master suite at the top of the house set aside for you. You could probably call it the honeymoon suite." She giggled in a very conspiratorial manner as she looked at them both.

"Would you like some help taking your bags up to the room?"

It was Marks turn to speak now.

"No we'll be fine thank you."

"You do look big and strong," she said, giving Mark a cursory glance up and down. Sara nudged him and gave him a wink, "Oh he is don't worry," and squeezed his arm.

The lady giggled again.

She continued to shuffle paper around behind the desk and write in various books and ledgers as she completed the checking in procedure. Mark watched and could only think that the waiting time here would have been greatly reduced if they had started to use a computer rather than relying on hard copies of everything. Besides, it seemed a little odd that they could advertise on the internet for a money off offer but not use any kind of computer system at the hotel proper. He was forming the thought to ask on the point when the lady thrust out her hand brandishing the single key and its large wooden fob for their room.

"Here you go you two. If you could just sign in here and we can get you up to your room."

Mark reached out for the pen on the desk and began to fill in the various details requested by the book. Strangely it included space for an e-mail address.

"When was the big day then?"

There it was, the question that they'd done some planning for but which still had the power to kick them both in their collective relaxation. They had known that they would be required to be married for less than a month to qualify for the offer and as such they had discussed briefly what they would say should the question be asked. And no sooner had the words left the lady's lips, Mark lost every last fragment of what they had discussed and was marooned holding the pen, trying his best to complete the gargantuan task of writing his name.

"Three weeks ago today." Sara had had no such problem holding onto the lie they had devised.

"Awful weather but we just didn't want to wait any longer." Sara beamed a megawatt smile as she completed the falsehood and hugged Marks arm to really sell the story. Judging by the look on the lady's face, his wife had sold it very well indeed.

"That's lovely. This big old place is so desperate for that kind of need in its love. When you just have to do something regardless of the details, it really is such a powerful force is love."

Sara nodded her agreement and Mark continued to fill in the form, breathing as quiet a sigh of relief as he could that his wife was such an adept liar. He never thought he'd have been happy to say that.

The knocking from the door behind the desk snapped everyone's attention away from the warmth of the happy feelings of love and longing which had been swirling around the whole reception area, instead bringing everyone back to a more washed out, unknown environment, all comfort somehow banished from sight.

"I told you to be still," shouted the old woman without turning around, an expression of anger tinged with nebulous apprehension playing across her face as she spoke.

The knocking stopped but not before there was one last bang, almost as an act of defiance from the other side of the wooden door.

"Just won't listen to me anymore."

Mark and Sara nodded together to show that they understood but they were both suddenly feeling far less comfortable in the whole situation. The best case was their host was going slowly round the twist and was talking to the wind as it crept its way through the cracks and imperfections of the house. The worst case could have gone pretty much anywhere.

Finally completing everything they needed to do, the lady explained the route they had to take to climb to their room, 'the crown jewel of the hotel', and they began the climb up the wide staircase. Their host had apologised for not having their bags taken up by blaming the effects of age on her back.

Step by creaking step they climbed, leaving the lady back down at the reception desk, feeling more than a little apprehensive of what would happen over the next two days. From below them, they could hear the lady complaining again that she wasn't being listened to. The banging had started up again but this time Sara was sure she could hear a whispering second voice answering back. Reaching the first floor balcony, they both looked over the bannister to check on the details of what was going on below them, shaken by what had happened as they checked in and wanting to identify what they had been hearing.

The wind continued to crash around outside the estate as they leaned carefully over the bannister to see that the lady was stood with her back to the desk, looking directly into the now open door at the back of the reception area. They both tried their best to make certain that they kept their presence a secret as they peered down on their host. The lady continued to speak regardless of the attention from above.

"You've got to keep out of sight. We can't have everyone who comes in here thinking that there are monsters making the doors rattle now, can we?"

Mark and Sara just looked at each other as they listened, neither really sure that they understood what was going on below them.

"She's crackers," was all that Mark could think to add to the thoughts that were being shared by the two.

He'd been aiming for a low whisper but his voice carried through the empty space of the hotel. The lady whipped her head up and stared directly at them, all the time trying desperately to close the door to wherever as fast as possible.

Mark and Sara snapped back away from the edge of the balcony area and hurried towards the next flight of stairs. They'd continue their conversation on the state of the place when they reached the veritable sanctuary of the room.

Pushing through the heavy door to the master suite of the hotel, they both felt a mixture of relief and growing trepidation. They were in the room so they would now at least be able to close the door against the creeping strangeness which was obviously running wild throughout the rest of the building but they were left with the realisation that they were, in the best meaning of the phrase, stuck here. The estate was stuck out in the middle of nowhere and there was no village that was within walking distance so they could nip out for a meal. As far as Mark could remember, the nearest village of any kind had been roughly ten miles away, and by the sounds of the wind which was still battering the outside world, any attempt to get there would be problematic at best and down-right life threatening at worst.

Dropping their bags on the bed as they clicked the door shut behind them, they were forced to accept that this weekend could just turn into staying in their room until it was time to check out. Anything was looking preferable to having to spend a huge amount of time interacting with the crazy receptionist again.

"I say again, I can see why they're offering such a massive discount." Sara was quick to get the ball rolling.

"Looked like you were building a close friendship down there. I was half expecting to have to send her a Christmas card every year from now on." Mark was now sprawled on the large double bed. What with the drive and the fun and games which had just unfolded downstairs, all he wanted to do was relax.

Sara kicked him.

"Come on, let's get everything sorted before we have a snooze."

Mark grunted his disapproval of the suggestion but heaved himself up on his elbows. It was only now that the pair had actually taken in the details of the room they were to be calling home for their time in Anngross House.

It was awful.

The whole place had been updated from the original decoration to include wallpaper and paintwork which was far more modern. Forty years ago. The original beams of the building were still exposed but they were now surrounded, not by gentle block colours of a subtle palette but instead by stark colours and wide swirling patterns in hues which were never designed to work together. A country house had just had the nineteen seventies be sick on it.

On all of the walls around the room, pictures of country vistas looked down between a showcase of questionable taxidermy. Animals which had once been foxes, squirrels, otters and stoats all stared out at the latest occupants of the room, their oddly shaped features highlighting the lack of skill which had created their poses in the afterlife. Directly above the bed was hung the masterpiece of the amateur stuffer, a stags head complete with a wide spray of antlers but missing one eye.

But that wasn't the worst part of the room's ensemble.

At the foot of the bed, on a small table framed with the utmost care, was a pair of china dolls, one dressed in exactly the same way as the lady who had greeted them downstairs, the other dressed as the high class country gent. Their glassy stares remained motionless, fixated on the head of the bed before them. Those dead eyes were set within faded china heads, both which had the cracks caused by the firing process, and chips, stains and blistering caused by great age. Their clothes were threadbare in the same way that the décor had been downstairs but the most off putting element of the dolls was how they had been posed. They had been set standing bolt upright with hands clasped behind their backs. They regarded them as a displeased headmistress and headmaster of the thirties may have done, all judgement and disappointment.

Mark and Sara had both been looking around the room in different directions but they had both fallen upon the objects together and they were both horrified at the visage.

"I'm not sleeping in here with those things staring at us." Sara made her feelings very clear. Mark was familiar with this kind of request. He had regularly had to deal with her dislike of toys, pictures and the like over the years so he knew there was no getting around what she was asking. That said, they were awful dolls and he would have suggested that they be moved even if Sara hadn't.

Mark scooped the two up and gently placed them in the nearest drawer of the unit with the TV on it. He'd been as careful as possible with them for fear of the things falling to bits in his hands.

As soon as the drawer was shut, the dolls secured away from the eyes of the guests, they were able to feel a fraction of relaxation creep over them. It was at that point that the banging started up.

Both Mark and Sara leapt in shock at the sound and struggled to pick out the origin point but it continued to boom into the room without giving them the chance. That solid sound of wood being impacted just tolled out its presence. They both stood up on opposite sides of the bed and tried to focus on the sound. It sounded like it was coming from the drawer.

"Will you stop playing around?" Sara folded her arms across her chest and stood on her left hip, looking at Mark, conveying her annoyance.

"I'm not doing anything," replied Mark, his hands in the air in a gesture of innocence.

"Then who's doing it then? Just make it stop so we can have a sleep." Sara sat back on the bed and scowled at the noise and at Mark who, it was clear, was the one behind it.

Sighing his resignation at the blame regardless of having nothing to do with it, he wandered towards the drawer, listening intently as the knocking continued relentlessly. It was only as he neared the drawer unit he could recognise that the sound wasn't coming from there but from the door to the room. Altering his step he strode confidently towards the front of the room, calling over his shoulder as he went, "It's the woman from downstairs. She's been banging on the door and we've been ignoring her because you thought it was me. Excellent."

He pulled the door open, already apologising for the delay in answering as it swung. She wasn't stood before him. He stopped mid-sentence and for that most delightful of split seconds just stood with his mouth open as he tried to work out what was going on.

Mark was quick to gather his wits back together and leaned out into the hallway beyond to see if there was anyone else who could have been making the noise.

Nothing.

"What's up now?" Sara had clearly had enough of whatever was going on.

"There's no-one out here," responded Mark, still looking left and right trying to understand what was happening.

"Just come to bed. We'll just ignore it if it happens again and complain about it to the lady downstairs when we go down for dinner." Sara had started to peel layers of clothing off and was determined to get some sleep. You'd swear that it had been her who'd driven them all of the way there. Resigning himself that there was either a very bored child or just a wind affected door to deal with, Mark pulled the door to and set about undressing to join his wife for an afternoon snooze.

Laying back, they closed their eyes and prepared for sleep.

The knocking began again.

Mark sighed and was up and out of the bed quickly, knowing that he would struggle to relax with that noise still carrying on.

Nothing outside again but there was also nowhere that anyone could have travelled before the door opened. The knocking was still happening when he turned the handle. Bored child theory ruled out then.

"It's the wind making the door rattle."

"Wonderful. Just jam some paper or something between the frame and door." Sara was getting grumpier by the second.

Three minutes later and the door was secure and Mark was back in bed, spooning up behind Sara.

"It is the honeymoon suite you know. We are the newlyweds who can't keep their hands off each other after all." He nuzzled against the back of her neck, his intentions perfectly clear.

Sara had other ideas.

"Go away. Let's just have a sleep. I'm tired."

"But, Honeymoon Suite." Mark persisted.

Sara had had enough.

"This may be the Honeymoon suite but we aren't newlyweds, remember? We've been married for years so just calm down, get over on your side of the bed and go to sleep."

That settled that and as they rolled apart both could feel a level of resentment at the other for what they perceived as unreasonable behaviour.

They fell asleep back to back and angry.

When the old lady finally forced the door open, it was Thursday.

The wind had settled down to what could be described as being a more seasonal average and there was a fragment of sun streaming in through the fractured cloud cover.

There hadn't been any further movement from Mark or Sara after they had checked in so she knew what that meant. Jamming the door open, she shuffled inside and spoke to the air as she did.

"It was clear that the offer was only for newlyweds, wasn't it?"

That tiny, source-less whispering hung in the air by way of response, more than just the wind outside.

"Did you get anywhere near enough?"

Silence this time.

The lady busied herself straightening the bed and re-making it, making everything as clean and tidy as possible. She casually re-packed the bags which had been left at the end of the bed, laying them ready to be taken down to the furnace when she'd finished.

As she was about to leave, she caught herself in the cool air, looking around for the something she had just noticed was missing.

"Where are you now?"

The slightest whisper.

"Oh my dear, we can't have you in there now can we?"

Moving with the hunched movements and pained gait which come with age, she ever so carefully removed the dolls from the drawer Mark had placed them in and lovingly straightened out the crumpled clothing, ensuring the arrangement was just perfect.

"You two have to go back on your pedestal don't you?"

She arranged the dolls back on the table they had originally been on and smiled.

"Maybe you can tell your new friends all about the power of real love."

She turned around, humming to herself, and pulled the door closed on the honeymoon suite.

Inside the room, the stillness returned and the air sat almost solid. The single eye from the stag's head looked out over the space with the same detached calm which had been there before Mark and Sara had entered the room.

It took in all of the details of the room, including the now four dolls with dead china faces, two dressed as old fashioned teachers and two wearing more modern garb, who stood on the end table, posed together forever.

Confession

I've heard on the radio, on TV and read in the press, of people making confessions and asking the wronged person for forgiveness many years after the event.

This is mine.

I can remember, more than a few years ago, when I was much smaller than I am today, my cousin and I never really saw eye to eye. She always had everything.

Everyone has the issue right? Not just us?

She's five years older than me and she was always the apple of our family's eye, nothing she did was ever wrong, even when it was and she was given everything her heart could ever want. I got the hand-me-downs.

Almost from my first childhood memory I heard, "Didn't you say that you wanted to have that as well?" asked by my parents as they passed down the latest object that she no longer wanted, gifted to them as a reminder that they weren't as good as my cousin's. It was almost worse than not having something myself, the cast offs.

Just looks like they were only ever thinking of me in terms of her rather than as being me.

So I don't think that it could have truly come as much surprise to anyone that jealousy built in me. I'm not proud of my jealousy but can you really say that if you'd been on the receiving end of behaviour like that for as long as I had, you wouldn't have been the same?

Eventually, after holding my younger self together for as long as I could, I'd had enough.

Visiting her house along with all manner of other people for a party or some kind of gathering in her honour, she was proudly showing off her latest prized possession, 'Little Ted'.

Little Ted was beautiful. Little Ted was made for cuddles and my smug cousin just looked down on me as I stood and stared at her with Little Ted.

I wanted my own Little Ted.

But that was never going to happen so I thought I'd do something about it.

As I've already said, I always got her cast offs when she didn't want them anymore, so I thought that now would be the perfect chance to take from her on my terms. I was the one doing the choosing.

I'm not proud of the way the green eyed monster grabbed hold of me but I just carried on with it.

There were just the three of us in the room when I decided I needed to act, she and I and Little Ted. I was going to take Little Ted for myself.

As the time passed by, all I could see was the fact I was going to have Little Ted. All of my rational mind was out of control, the green eyed monster now truly in charge.

Eventually, she was no doubt distracted by something else that she had that I didn't as she played to others who were there, I saw my chance.

I bundled up Little Ted and hid him up my jumper.

Turning quickly, I walked out of the house, not meeting her eyes as I left. Surely she'd be able to see that I had something under my jumper as I left? Maybe if she'd been a little less self absorbed, she would have done.

Happily for me, she noticed Little Ted was missing after I'd left the house.

I heard that she'd cried and cried and cried.

I'm still not proud of the fact that I'd taken from her but she did need to see that she couldn't just have everything she ever wanted and rub it in the faces of all around her.

But,

I wasn't really sure, as I looked at Little Ted later in the day, that I actually wanted him.

I was scared that I'd be discovered as the taker.

So this is my confession after all these years.

I'm sorry I ruined your life.

I'm sorry I took your Little Ted.

I just wanted to show you that what it was like not to have everything go your way.

I tell you this now for closure for us both.

How was I supposed to know that after that day your marriage would fall apart, that you couldn't have any more kids.

So twenty years later, your son Edward, your Little Ted, is buried in the woods by our old house.

Make Believe Friend

It's been said that being a parent of a child who is going through the 'terrible two's' is akin to attempting to placate and cajole a hurricane. Parents the world over have been swept aside by the battering they receive of constant howling screams, prized possessions being hurled around with absolute abandon and the constant knowledge that at any time, it could get even worse. But why are the two's so terrible?

Walking backwards, very slowly and deliberately, from her son's bedroom, Sam could practically feel the rain water from the latest appearance of 'Hurricane George' dripping from her hair. Step by step, inch by inch, she made her way away from the now dormant form of her son and towards the relative safety of the world beyond those four walls. She managed to avoid all of the scattered toys which had threatened to impede her path and even steered clear of the now infamous, 'squeaky floorboard by the door'. Both Sam and her husband Jeff had been caught out by the floorboard in the past. Just when they had started to feel they were in the clear, they hit the board by the door and George was awake and looking for trouble, his angelic looking golden curls mussed in such a way as to cover completely the devil horns he must have sprouted by now.

Step by gingerly placed step, she eased out of the room and slowly pulled the door closed, running through the same deliberate movements to make absolutely sure there was no way George could be disturbed. Finally, with the barest hint of a click, the door was closed and she could breathe a silent sigh of relief.

Letting her shoulders sag at the sudden release of tension she had been holding in every muscle and sinew of her body, she padded slowly down the hallway and headed back down stairs to curl back up with Jeff. As Sam walked hurriedly back into the living room, keen to settle back down to gentle relaxation, Jeff looked up from scrolling through the TV guide.

"I don't know how you keep so calm?" he shook his head slowly and patted the sofa next to him, raising his arm in a gesture of beckoning. Sam settled back into the nook of his arm and felt great swathes of tension wash away.

"I had to get out before I started screaming myself." Jeff continued and kissed the top of her head.

"Don't panic Jeff. Just save your energy, you're going in on your own next time." Sam looked up at her husband and could feel the almost primal dread shoot through him. She giggled and nudged him in the side. She knew she could never do that to him. She'd definitely leave him in there on his own but they would always start out as a team.

Turning the TV back on, at a very low volume of course, she took one look at the baby monitor which was stood on the coffee table, the modern day equivalent of the master ringing a bell to attract the attention of a servant. Crossing her fingers that George would sleep for at least ten hours, she could make out the gentle rhythmic breathing sounds her son was making. Everything was settling down again, and Sam closed her eyes and allowed herself to drift with the sounds of her sleeping son.

The noise from the baby monitor made her frown.

It wasn't enough to really draw her full attention but, it was there none the less. Then it happened again, but this time, just a little louder.

"Did you hear that Jeff?" she asked, opening her eyes to look at the monitor.

"Hear what?" replied Jeff, not taking his eyes from the TV.

The sound came again and this time Sam sat up and lent forwards towards the small device. George could still be heard, snoring a little now, but she was certain there was more than just his slumber being transmitted to the unit. Sam tugged Jeff forwards with her and muted the TV.

"On the monitor. It sounded like a giggle." She was straining to strip away every other sound which was adding to what was taking place above her in her son's bedroom, piece by piece ruling out noise after noise.

"He's probably having a funny dream," added Jeff in way of explanation, quickly adding, "He's probably laughing at us. Thinking about how much trouble he seems to be causing and having a good laugh at our expense." Sam elbowed Jeff but smiled to herself. George always did find the frazzled expressions on his parent's faces to be the funniest thing in the world, like he was being egged on by them feeling worse.

Sam started to relax back into the sofa; wrapping one leg over Jeff's to get comfortable for the night. The calm didn't last.

The monitor crackled and popped gently and the sound of rushing air could be heard spitting from the speaker. Then the giggle came again, but this time much louder and accompanied by a hissing, breathing call of "Georgie".

Sam and Jeff were out of the sofa and surging up the stairs in seconds. Gone was any pretence of not waking the baby as they rushed towards the baby's room and the source of the strange sounds.

Throwing the door open they turned the light on and were stopped still in the centre of the room by the sight that greeted them.

George was stood in his cot with a broad smile on his face, clapping his hands as he jumped up and down and shrieked with laughter. On the floor of his bedroom, less than two feet from the triumphant toddler, was the broken casing of the baby monitor, its innards spilling out like a macabre electronic murder scene amongst the other scattered toys.

Sam rushed forwards and scooped up their son while Jeff checked that the window was still closed and there wasn't anyone under, behind, on top of or in any of the furniture. As Sam watched him track through the room and find nothing at all out of the ordinary, she felt more at ease. George continued to howl with laughter the whole time this search took place.

When Jeff started to look inside the drawers of the table and chairs play set they'd bought George last Christmas, Sam couldn't help herself and she started to smile. Jeff noticed and realised what he was doing was probably a little excessive. He straightened himself up and looked at Sam, to report his findings.

"All clear in here. Nothing out of the ordinary."

That almost felt worse. Looking at their son who was now calming down but who still had a huge, open-mouthed grin, the couple began to run through the facts as they could see them.

George was still in his cot when they entered the room. As far as they were aware, there was no way he was able to climb out of the bed let alone return to it after having made his way out. The smashed baby monitor was not only on the other side of the room from the cot, it was also on top of a five foot high chest of drawers, well out of the reach of their sons tiny grasping hands. The unit was battery operated so there was no trailing wire to be reached for and there was no object that could have been pushed into place and used as a boost for their son to reach up from.

Sam looked at Jeff but there was no answer coming from either of them. George hadn't smashed the monitor because he couldn't get to it. There was no-one else in the room who could have done the deed, they would have been seen, yet they had both heard that voice saying their sons name, George giggling away to himself about something and then the wrecked monitor.

"What about the voice on the monitor?" Sam wanted to know where that odd voice had come from.

"Probably picking up something from a TV or radio around here. God knows what the range of that thing really is." Jeff was very matter of fact about the whole situation.

"But it said Georgie, Jeff."

"It sounded like Georgie. It could have been any number of things. We haven't got to worry about an evil ghost coming to play with our son; your mother's still alive."

Sam snorted a laugh of her own but her unease remained.

"He's coming back downstairs with us and he's sleeping with us tonight." Sam's tone told Jeff not to argue, this was a statement of fact. Decision made, they both turned and headed out of the door, Sam with George bundled up in her arms with his head rested on her shoulder, Jeff picking up a few stuffed toys for George to play with.

Just as Jeff switched off the light, George let out a short laugh and waved back into the room, "Bye bye Mimp".

The two adults looked each other, wondering what he was on about but thought he must be talking about a toy that he had seen but hadn't made it through the selection process for the journey downstairs. The walked on and George continued to wave over his mother's shoulder, repeating over and over again, "Mimp, Mimp, Mimp, Mimp".

Back downstairs, Sam and Jeff struggled to get their son to settle down and go back to sleep. They each took turns waiving different toys at him but he wasn't even remotely interested in anything that was presented. They tried different DVD's. Time after time, the colourful cartoons or dancing men in silly animal suits failed to draw his attention. Time and again, he turned away from the options presented to him and all he could be heard saying was, again, "Mimp, Mimp, Mimp."

"I'll go and find this bloody 'Mimp' toy of his. He may not be getting tired but I'm knackered," said a haggard Jeff.

"Do you even know which one is Mimp?" asked an equally exhausted Sam, dropping her head back to stretch her neck as George wriggled in her lap. They both looked down at George and tried to think. Which toy did George call Mimp?

It didn't sound like a real name of a toy they had bought him so it must be one he had given himself. They both mulled over the multitude of options, trying to work out who Mimp was.

"MIMP!" shouted George with a delighted smile on his face. He cranked up his wriggling and started to moan.

Sam had had enough by now so let him go. They both watched as he toddled his way towards the doorway and happily sat down in front of it. The door opened into the room, next to the sofa they were both sat on. Looking down on their son he finally seemed happy to stare into the hallway beyond and gurgle and giggle to himself.

"Finally!" said Jeff and relaxed back into the sofa.

"George, you OK?" Sam wanted to make sure before she even dared relax. George nodded back at her, grinning all of the time.

"Finally!" Sam agreed.

George spent the next twenty minutes staring out into the hallway, jabbering to himself. He would occasionally wander towards his toys and take one back with him but other than that he was content to amuse himself. The DVD's of all the kids programmes were put away and Sam and Jeff started to watch a film which was more to their taste. Gradually, the mood of the evening started to calm down as everyone in the house could relax and enjoy what was going on. Sam was always keeping one eye on George but he seemed content so all was fine.

Then it moved at the edge of her vision.

Snapping her head to focus fully at he son, Sam watched in shocked disbelief as a small, jet black, leathery hand reached out and touched her sons face. Her blood froze and all the sound of horror and fear were jammed solid in her throat. What was sat on the other side of the door?

She tried to move but before the impulse had passed to her muscles, the hand gripped Georgies romper suit and dragged him forward, behind the open door and into the darkened hallway beyond.

George screamed.

That sound was enough to shatter the spell of fear which had been gripping Sam. She burst to her feet and steamed out of the room, Jeff not far behind.

Flicking the switch, the hallway was bathed in the diffuse light from the overhead fittings. George stood still in the centre of the hallway, holding hands with, something. Their once angelic son was different. On his face was an expression which he had never had before. It could only be described as being malevolent. His brow was furrowed and his eyes were full of anger. All this on top of his wide smile created a vision to be truly unnerved by.

And both he and the something were holding very large kitchen knives.

Sam skidded to a stop and tried to take in the detail of what she was seeing. It was only now that she really looked at who was holding her sons hand. It was small; roughly the same height as George, but it was black skinned. It wasn't wearing any clothes and had no hair anywhere on its body. It stood with a hunched back and its spindly limbs jutted out, almost painfully, from an emaciated body.

As Sam took in more and more of the detail, it slowly tightened its grip on Georges hand with its own taloned appendage and a wide, serrated toothed grin spread across its face under its sparkling blood red eyes.

Jeff leaned over Sam's shoulder, also piecing the details together. He gripped tightly to her arms as the situation settled on him.

Sam spoke first.

"Who's your friend George?" She tried her best to keep the fear out of her voice and raised her hands in a gesture of non-aggression.

George didn't move, but hissed, "Mimp."

Mimp shook his head and turned his head to face George. Its voice was like broken glass.

"Mummy. Daddy. Just like all little children, Georgie included, I want to play. Do you want to play with us?"

The final 's' was elongated into the sound a snake might make if it had been granted the power of speech.

"Georgie. Are you OK honey?" was all Sam could think to ask. She tried to put the little thing holding his hand out of her mind as being something she was making up but she still had to get the knife out of his grasp. George nodded at her and his smile seemed to grow wider as he started to chant the name Mimp over and over again, his head bobbing around excitedly as he did.

Mimp spoke again. "We should play a game. Let's play doctors and nurses." Again, the final syllable was stretched out as the thing spoke and caused the wave of icy fear to roll over Sam.

Mimp slowly turned towards Georgie and started to raise the almost comically over-sized kitchen knife in a gesture of slow attack. Jeff was fast to move.

Sam was only able to utter a sound rather than a word as her husband took two quick, reaching strides across the space between the two pairs and made a sweeping grab at the knife being wielded by the 'it'.

Without there seeming to have been any movement at all from the two smaller bodies, light glinted from the whirling blades of the pair and Jeff let out a startled yelp of pain and slid past his intended target, collapsing into a pile on the floor behind them, breathing hard. Blood was starting to spread out across the fabric he wore around the now multiple slash marks where the knives had casually, and far too swiftly, sliced through both material and flesh.

Jeff scrambled himself round so he was facing the two but just lay, still grimacing through the pain.

"Doctor. Daddy is hurt. How do we make the pain stop?" Mimp's voice held a small giggle under all of the shards of speech it was capable of. Georgie kept grinning as he looked round at his father and slowly lifted the knife.

"That's right Georgie. Let's make all of daddy's pain go away."

"Wait," was all Sam could think to shout. She had to stop her son doing something to her husband, while stopping the thing doing anything to either of them, all the while trying to protect herself as well.

Georgie kept his eyes intently on his father as Mimp turned back to face Sam.

"Does Mummy want her pain taken away first? Does Mummy hurt?" The red eyes narrowed in its inky face and it tilted its head to regard her in a way that paralysed Sam to the spot. That fear was so primal that it had managed to rush straight past the rational parts of her mind and hit her in the unguarded sections of her psyche, rooting her to the spot.

She had to move fast or this little horror was going to be more than able to hurt them all, or worse.

"I want to play a new game. Don't you?" she stammered.

Mimp considered that for a brief second and then its own smile started to widen in pleasure.

"Yes, yes, yes. What game?" It started to bob around much like Georgie did when he got excited, obviously eager to start a new playtime. Georgie even turned back to his mother and started to smile. He looked more like himself now, humour replacing threat.

"What games do you like?" Sam asked with a quivering voice. "How do I know what games you like the most to make it the most fun it can be?"

"All games are fun. All games are fun. I do love musical statues," it spoke excitedly and in a blur, streaked back towards Jeff. Jeff screamed out in hot pain as Mimp plunged the kitchen knife deeply into his flank. He dropped the heavy ornamental dragon he had been easing towards the monster with and slumped back down on the floor, now with much more blood seeping from him. Before Sam could do or say anything, Mimp was back across the gap to Georgie and was taking his hand again.

"I love it when people are still in games. Moving is cheating." Mimps eyes bored into Sam.

"What games don't you like to play?" She had to keep her composure. Looking up briefly at Jeff she could see that he was placing as much pressure on the latest wound as possible.

"I love all games. All games are fun." Mimp was jumping up and down at this point clapping his hands at the sheer delight of new play mates. Georgie, though, wasn't. Instead her son was now standing looking a little confused. The smile was still there but he looked a little lost. The knife had also dropped from a ready position to now having the tip on the floor.

Then it dropped from his hand and Georgie started to toddle towards his mother, arms outstretched and the smile slowly receding.

Mimp was quick to notice and swiftly grabbed Georgies hand again. The action immediately stopped the child's forward motion and in the passing of a handful of heartbeats, the wicked smile had returned to Georgie's face and he had started to reach back for the knife he had dropped.

Sam was quick to register the significance of the action. All she needed to do to break the spell of the creature was break its physical contact with Georgie and he would likely return to being the little boy she knew and loved.

Just, how to do that.

Sam settled herself as much as possible and tried to regain what little composure she had worked together.

"Who are you Mimp? What do you want? To play?" She had to keep it focussed on her and try to engineer the release of its grip on her son.

Both Mimp and Georgie adjusted their respective grips on their weapons as Mimp spoke.

"I am an Imp. We all like to play games, make jokes, have fun. Georgie likes to have fun too that's why I'm here." That made Sam think.

"How did you know that Georgie likes to play games?" The more focus the Imp had on her the better and she was starting to get more information about the creature.

"I watched him. I spoke with him and we played together. He likes to play tricks doesn't he?" With the last word of the sentence the imp tilted its head and hardened its gaze, almost challenging Sam to disagree with it. She was running out of time and she knew the creature was aware of it.

"How did you speak to him? Why didn't you speak to me? I like to play games." Sam continued without giving the imp the chance to move from the conversation.

"Mummies and Daddies don't listen to us. We have to speak to kiddies. They're the only ones who really want to play so we come in to rooms through mirrors and talk to them. Georgie and I are going back so we can keep playing." Sam could feel the immediate rise of an overwhelming panic at the last comment.

"Why would you want to take my son?" asked Sam and she knew that her terror had come leaking through as she had spoken.

The imp smiled back and narrowed his eyes even further. "He's mine now."

The attack that followed was swifter than anything Sam could have thought possible and hit with the strength of a car crash. Jeff had continued his slow, shuffling progress towards the imp and had brought the ornate piece of sculpted stone down on the head of the imp.

The shock and undoubted pain of the attack slammed through the imp and it dropped the knife it had been brandishing and relinquished the grip it had had on Georgie. It had been given no opportunity to respond in any way and was hammered to the floor.

Jeff continued to swing and bash at the little monster, mashing more and more of it across the floor of the hallway in a gore filled paste. Thick grey blood and chunks of black flesh were split and spilt everywhere as Jeff yelled his own defiance.

Thunderous blow after thunderous blow landed and pulverised the target. What little movement had come from the imp soon stopped and there was soon very little to show that it had ever been anything other than a revolting pile of parts in an awful puddle.

Sam rushed forwards and scooped Georgie up into her arms, knocking the knife away as far as she could. Running quickly away from what Jeff was doing, she could see that Georgie's face was turning back from the mask of anger to a startled, fearful expression of someone who wasn't sure what was going on around him. He started to grizzle and Sam bathed in the relief that brought.

"It's dead," called Jeff from the hallway. Sam rocked Georgie, attempting to calm him. She shushed him as gently as she could and slowly edged back towards the hall, making sure to keep her son facing away.

The hallway had now been coated in the entrails of the imp. Jeff was slumped back on the floor clutching tightly to his side where he had been stabbed by the imp. The blood was free flowing again and by the almost empty pallor on his face he needed medical attention and he needed it quickly.

Looking at the mess Jeff had made of the imp, Sam let out the tension of the ordeal and set about bundling her family into the car before heading off to the hospital at break neck speed.

Jeff was quickly seen to by the nurses who rushed him through for surgery. Sam was asked on more than one occasion how he had been injured but each time she trotted out the story she had concocted. He had fallen down stairs in the garden at home while they had been moving a collection of old tools they were going to throw away. Every person she told the story to had the same expression on their face when they left but there was no further argument.

Eventually she was left alone in a small waiting room with Georgie bundled up in a blanket sleeping on the sofa next to her. He was breathing smoothly and snored just a little bit. Sam looked down on her son and felt that she could relax. Closing her eyes she let herself drift slowly and slip into a warm sleep, one hand resting gently on her sons back.

Here mind was filled with flashback images of the encounter they had all had. Dreams of flashing knives, scarlet glowing eyes, black leathery skin and that inhuman voice rebounded around her mental landscape, until,

"We liked the game, playing dead. That was fun, oh yesssssssss."

She snapped awake with a renewed sense of terror churning in her stomach. Her hand was still resting on the blanket but now Georgie was no longer in it.

"Georgie," she called into the small room, pleading that he had just climbed down to toddle around but there was no answer. She frantically searched the few spaces in the room that her son could have hidden behind and again found nothing. She was just about to leave the room and scream for the nurses, porters, doctors, anyone who could have seen Georgie when her eyes fell across the mirror which was looking back at her. The mirror and the two shapes which were staring back at her from behind her in the room.

The imps red eyes beamed back at her and she could see that it was holding hands with Georgie again.

Sam turned to reach for the boy from his position on the back of the sofa but was greeted by nothing as she turned. They weren't there. Looking back to the mirror, they hadn't moved so she checked again but there was nothing.

Then she looked into the mirror and saw the truth.

"We come in through mirrors," screamed in her head in the same broken glass voice the imp had used at the house and a terrible realisation hit her. They were *in* the mirror.

"We're going to play now. Bye bye mummy," creaked the imp and beckoned to Georgie.

Sam thrust her hands out to the mirror but they slapped uselessly against the cold surface. She stared deeply at her sons face which was again contorted into a rictus grin but the eyes looking back at her were now a deep red.

"Bye bye mummy," slithered out of Georgie's mouth and Sam started screaming, beating her hands against the mirror until it fell to the floor and smashed into hundreds of irregular shards. Lifting each piece in turn Sam checked for the reflection image of her son and the imp but in each there was nothing but the room around her.

The imp was gone now but it had taken a new friend.

Remember, parents, when you think that your child is becoming more mischievous and is turning into a little monster, there may be something whispering into their ear that they should really be playing a game.

Always check under the beds and behind the cupboards. Never underestimate what could be lurking in the shadows and, always, always watch out for the mirrors.

Mountain Pass

I hate going to see my family.

Is it the same for everyone that the long journey to meet them acts as just a drawn out pause before you are forced to take the mighty first step from the plane?

Every second of that trip to what had once been 'home' grows into a tortured lifetime as you run through the various scenarios that have happened in the past and will probably be discussed throughout the whole time you're there. The same old issues and arguments, the same old disappointments will be waiting in the house along with your parents, ghosts whispering into ears and guiding the animosity for everyone.

By the time you're ready to leave, every nerve will have been plucked and every last ounce of shared indifference and shame would have been purposefully dragged into the daylight, all becoming the sour taste of unspoken resentment which you leave with and which then wraps itself around yet more memories.

Like I said, I hate going to see my family.

I live roughly three hundred miles from my parents so don't have to see them that regularly but when I can't put the journey off any more, I am forced to drive for over five hours to do my penance. Talk about paying for the privilege of being beaten.

So here I am, piloting myself on that most dreaded of trips. I'm sending myself into a place where I will be compared with friends of the family in terms of job status, income, partner, marriage prospects, savings plans, hobbies, and, even in my thirties, choice of clothes. There really was nothing pleasant to come from these trips. The late autumn day was ticking on as I drove. The day was bright, but crisp, the early touch of the icy fingers of winter reaching out as far as they could.

Ahead of me, the roadway bobbed and weaved through the gently undulating countryside. Despite it being the twenty first century and modern roadways providing an almost disturbingly direct connection to large swathes of the country, the fastest route for me to take was off the pristine, super fast motorways and onto the slightly less inspiring routes of what I would describe as being the large country road. They're much bigger than the stereotypical winding country track, having wide lanes, intermittent crash barriers and even road markings but they are none the less constrained by the geography they are traversing. No Roman inspired straight lines for these vehicular arteries. These routes don't make the land bend to their will; rather it's the hills that call the shots. Curl after twist after gentle bend push the road into different patterns and the route takes on the appearance of spaghetti post boiling rather than the pre boiled motorways.

As the line of traffic I was a part of made its stuttering way over mile after mile of tarmac which looked totally at odds with the rest of the landscape, my mind started to pick out the main topic points which would always seem to find their way into discussion. Working through the issues I was trying to prepare my defences against the enemy sorties. "Did you know that Chris' daughter has had another promotion. She's some kind of National Director in her firm now. £150,000 a year now. She must have a lovely house," said Mum. "Your old girlfriend Debbie has just had her third child. Her third girl. You made such a lovely couple when you were together. Are you and Sandra going to ever have kids?" said Dad. "Working in an insurance company, you should be the boss by now. Have you done something so people don't look at you as management material? I was running four departments by the time I was thirty. You've got some catching up to do, haven't you?" said Mum.

Every choice that I had made over the years had been disputed and scrutinized ad nauseum. My view on the world and attempts to function within it were held up to the cold, hard glare of parental disdain on an almost daily basis. My every decision on the who's, where's and why's of me were scowled at, had heads shaken at them and were seen as needing correction.

In moments of empathy, I tried to put myself into the shoes of my parents and view me through their eyes. Looking at my life as my parents allowed me to always understand the same fact. I was happy in the life I was leading. I wasn't destitute even though I was only a low level bod in the company I worked for. I lived with a beautiful woman and we enjoyed our time together. Sandra and I holidayed in far off places, we could have lazy lay ins on a Sunday morning and we always managed to avoid having clothes with sick on them. My life was exactly what I wanted for it. My parents though had far reaching expectations for me which had nothing to do with either my capabilities or my desires. The ball of perceived missed opportunities must have been wound so tight in each of their stomachs.

Shaking my mind back to the road ahead of me, I quickly realized that I had been driving on autopilot for far too long. My gambits of verbal warfare slid back from the front of my mind and for the first time in what seemed like a month and what was probably at least twenty five miles and a large slice of the light of dusk, I actually watched the road rather than just drifting with it and trusting to memory.

The sun had almost completely been dragged down below the horizon and it was pulling all of the remaining light down after it, a thin sheet of glowing material which had touched everything but which was now being pulled from the table as if by a petulant child.

Checking my mirrors and giving myself a metaphorical slap across the face, I brought myself back to the journey at hand. Passing by a fading road sign proclaiming this road to be an accident black spot created in my mind the view of my mother wagging her finger at me. Jesus, concentrate.

Along with the sun, all of the other cars that had been with me as the motorized parts of the segmented body of a caterpillar, were now gone. I pondered the fact that those people were doing the same as me, all heading to a family meeting that they would truly rather avoid or if they were now being welcomed with open arms into the womb like comfort of a family unit that loved and respected each other.

I shook that image away as I had the planning session earlier. Stop your mind wandering for God's sake.

The last of the light was slipping from sight now and the relatively low temperature from the day would soon be falling even lower during the night. Turn after turn passed by and the journey continued.

Night had soon fallen fully and I could feel the cold piercing into the car through vents, cracks and any number of other places. Outside, there was a low, patchy fog starting to lift from the vegetation covered ground on either side of the road. I'd run through intermittent clouds which ranged from barely a whisp to those which completely obscured everything from view. My pace was being slowed by these foggy obstacles but at least I was more aware of what was going on around me, all thoughts of my familial warfare or lack of happy homecoming gone.

Rounding a long bend very slowly as the fog tumbled down the hillside to meet me I could feel an irrational fear looking over my shoulder, whispering a rising dread. Outside the car, the surroundings were taking on a distinctly ominous feel.

The fog grew thicker.

My pace slowed even further.

The road visible ahead of me was being eaten away despite the best efforts of my full beam lights. I was being surrounded by a fog which was so thick as to almost have mass. If I had reached out into it I could have lifted up a handful. Grey tasteless candy floss being poured onto the roadway and everything on it.

My rational mind was steadfastly repeating that this was just a natural phenomenon and that I should grow up but the fear centres of my brain were beginning to shout even louder. They had started to point out the dangers of driving in conditions like this, how the slightest wrong turn or miscalculation of speed could turn a solid road into the free fall down the hillside but as the fog continued to engulf the car more and more thoughts of monsters in the fog, demons of pain, ghosts and practically every horror film stereotype known to mankind had been fighting for my attention.

My visibility was now down to practically nothing and my speed fell even further. This was getting beyond ridiculous. How long would this last? How long would I be delayed? Should I just stop and wait for it to clear?

I tried to work out my best options when, almost at the snap of a higher powers fingers, the fog was behind me.

I had burst through to the other side of an incredibly low cloud and the road ahead was totally clear. I could feel that I had just pulled that delightful 'surprise' expression we all seem to pull when we get startled by a loud noise or someone jumps out on us. The immediacy of the clarity of road was a touch shocking.

That and the woman in white standing in the centre of the carriageway with the same expression on her face.

We've all been there. Confronted by a situation which requires a huge shift from the moment of shocked surprise to actually doing something because of the nature of the surprise. In so many cases these situations seem to occur in a car. A child, animal, other road user appears and we have to make a split second decision as to the correct outcome.

As quickly as my mind could process the information which was ahead of me I came to the conclusion that I had three options.

I could swerve to avoid her, turning right. That would force me to turn towards the elevated hill side of the road, in short, meaning I would be turning into a natural wall.

I could swerve to avoid her, turning left. No wall this time so that was a plus but instead a very large drop down the valley side. Not so positive.

I could jam the brakes on hoping to stop before I hit her. My very low speed traveling through the fog and my intense desire not to crash my car in the middle of nowhere made it an easy choice.

The car responded quickly to my hurried request to stop. I swear it had weighed up the alternatives in the same way I had and it had come to the same conclusion. I think it may have done it faster than me.

The nose of my car dipped down as I applied the brakes as fast as I could.

I stopped in plenty of time but the resulting recoil and suspension bounce from the car did blast bright fog light into the woman's eyes and managed to keep her terror going even further.

Hazards on, I ventured out to, well I'm not sure what I was going to do but I was going to give it a go anyway, anything less after almost running someone down did seem to be a bit rude. Maybe my parent's obsession with always being polite to everyone and always 'going the extra mile' was worthwhile after all?

"Are you OK?" I asked into the cold night air. My breath was forming clouds ahead of me, caught on a gentle, sporadic breeze which was hopping around the car. Exhalation after exhalation was caught in the grip and pulled back in the direction of the fog, as if rejoining the fluffy mass which it had been pulled from. The woman blinked and seemed to struggle to see where the sound had come from. She cast a glassy stare all around her, as if searching for the origin of the noise. I started to move slowly towards her and asked again.

"I said, are you OK?" She still didn't seem to be fully registering much beyond the fact she could hear something. It didn't look like she could even pick out what the individual words were. No meaning, just sound.

She was wearing a long flowing white dress which looked more suitable for a warm summer evening than a cold night on the hillside. Her long red hair was loose and fell onto her shoulders in the delightfully undone fashion of those who don't try but still look better than those who do. I knew very little about the finer points of female hairstyles but even I could see that she looked distressed. She had on thin, slip on shoes and no coat or jacket. Her skin had started to dimple in the cold and she was pale as all blood rushed away from her skin's surface.

Walking slowly towards her, the harsh beams of my car's headlights catching her in a prison of their castings, I tried to show her that I was there to help.

"Where have you come from?" I couldn't see a car anywhere but it was more than believable that I had just driven past it in the fog without even registering its presence. She steadily turned her head to face me, again following the sound rather than actually registering what was being said to her. Her breathing was shallow and it looked as if she was waging a war within herself, fear and relief each fighting for the upper hand. What had she seen or gone through to be feeling this way?

"I need to go home."

Her voice had been a cracked whisper and she had seemed to struggle with what she had said. She had only managed to speak five words but in that short sentence she had conveyed so much. I knew that she needed me to help.

Her eyes were wide and she trembled as I regarded her.

"Where's home?" Start with the easy stuff. She was still breathing very quickly as she stared at me. My own deep breaths were forming and being caught by the wind to be carried still towards the fog while hers were creating no sign of steam that I could make out.

What was going on?

She looked into me hard without blinking, all the time still trembling. There were no more words from her as we looked at each other. I willed her to tell me where she was from but nothing was coming.

"Do you come from that way?" I encouraged as I pointed out down the road away from the direction I had come from. She nodded slightly in affirmation.

"Would you like me to take you home? I can give you a lift if you want. Is there anyone you want to call?" I offered my phone but one quick glance at the screen showed that I had no signal.

"Come on, I'll give you a lift, you'll catch your death out here." There was a sharp intake of breath but she did start to edge her way towards the passenger side of the car. Progress.

I opened the door for her and she slid into the seat, all the while keeping a nervous gaze on me. She looked around the car as she fastened the belt, taking in all of the detail she could. This was very strange.

Turning to head back towards the driver's side, I looked back behind the car and for the first time noticed that the fog was still as thick as it had been behind us. The glow of the red lights from the car and the intermittent flashes from the hazards were illuminating an almost solid wall of fog. It was utterly still behind the car and, despite the breeze that I could feel, was showing no signs of dissipating.

I needed to get the both of us off the hillside and back to civilization.

Climbing back into the car and starting the engine I turned the heater up to full blast, she must have been frozen out there. All the while, there was no movement from my passenger. No noise or change in temperature was registering and as I pulled the car away, she remained staring blankly out of the windscreen. I was able to get back to the more normal speed you would expect to reach on a road like this now the air around us was clear of fog. Overhead there was a bright moon casting even more light over everything.

"What's your name? Can you tell me your name?" I needed to try to engage her in some form of conversation otherwise I may never know where she wanted to go. She kept her gaze focused firmly on the road ahead but at least managed to answer.

"I'm Jane. I need to get home."

Jane. That was something. "What were you doing all the way up on the hill? Are you OK?"

"There was an accident. I need to get home."

"An accident?" Was she hurt? Had she seen something? I needed to know more. She didn't respond.

"What accident?" I asked her a little more forcefully. She snapped her head round to face me, startled by the question.

"I need to get home. Please take me home." I could hear the soon to be flowing tears in her voice.

"Ok Jane." Let's just drive until she calms down a little and see what we can find out.

"I'll just drive until we come across where you were going. If you need me to change the way I'm going, just let me know. By the way, my name's Hugo."

"Please take me home," she croaked limply, the sound almost too scared to venture forwards, "My mum is expecting me home." She was still staring blankly out ahead of us, still not really registering anything which was going on around her.

Looking ahead, I turned my full attention back to the road. Sighing to myself I started to kick around different options for starting some kind of conversation with Jane. I couldn't just drive in the hope that I would be lucky enough to stumble on where she wanted to go. Knowing my luck I'd either get lost trying to find a hospital or police station, either that or I'd end up taking her home with me. God I could just imagine my parents' faces as they looked into the car.

Let's give it another go.

"Where were you heading tonight?" If in doubt, start with the basics.

Jane didn't turn to look at me but did answer the question.

"I'm going to see my family. I've just got back from holiday."

"Been anywhere nice?" Try to appear casual despite relief she was starting to respond to me.

"Spain. Very warm."

Well that at least explained what she was wearing.

"Did you go alone or with family?" Now to build on the fact that she was warming to me.

"I need to get to my parents, please, I need to get to my parents." Her bottom lip was starting to quiver wildly as she spoke and a desperation had crept into her voice. She remained looking ahead but I could see that she was trembling.

My action was instinct. She was in pain and all I wanted to do was reassure her. I wanted to show her that she was safe with me and that I wanted to look after her. I reached out and took her hand.

The contact between us was there for just an instant but it shocked both of us. She had not been expecting the touch of my hand and recoiled from it. I though, hadn't been expecting the ice cold feel of her skin. She was beyond cold, her skin feeling more akin to raw fillets of chicken, her skin had a waxy touch to it.

Gathering myself as much as I could, all I could focus my mind on was the fact that she felt as if all life had left her.

My eyes were flicking around the car quickly trying to take in any and all details I could to reassert rational thinking. Jane was now leaning very far from me and was pressed up against the passenger door, still staring intently out of the windscreen.

My mind was still racing with images of all kinds of spectral horrors but I needed to get to the bottom of what was going on.

"Don't worry, I'll get you there but I need to know where I'm going." Back to the same argument.

"I need to make up with my parents." She continued with the same thoughts she had regardless of my last comment or actions.

"We argued the last time we spoke and I need to make things right with them. Please take me home."

Taking a deep breath I steadied myself, gripping onto the steering wheel before I moved at the conversation again. Despite the fear in me, I could hear in her the exact core of my own feeling. Despite always moaning to myself about the horrors that these trips to see my family would contain I did want to have a relaxed relationship with them. I could understand the need to clear the air before too much time had passed. I could recognize in Jane so many elements of myself. We had both obviously done things which our parents had deemed to be unacceptable or disappointing in some way. The difference between us was that Jane had decided to correct the issue which had squatted between her and her family, I had simply been content to let the stain in my family fester unchecked. My family had been happy to simply pretend that the problems weren't actually there, instead easing behind masks of convenient platitudes as a way of easing our collective travels through our interactions.

Looking inwards I could see that I needed to make peace with my own family.

"Please take me home. I need to see my parents." Jane was repeating the same line over and over again.

I had picked up a woman in white on a foggy mountain road after she has been involved in an unnamed accident. She was desperate to reach her destination and seemed to be unresponsive to everything I had to say outside of the most rudimentary information. She also didn't look or feel very well. We've all heard stories of people picking up ghostly hitch-hikers and how they all needed to get to a set destination, one they had been unable to reach in life. I never thought that I'd have a ghost in my car. I needed to get her to her destination as fast as I could. That and make sure I didn't wet myself out of sheer reflex.

"Where do you want me to take you?" I needed to get her to at least tell me where she needed to go. That's what you should do with the ghosts in these stories right?

Jane was still staring blankly ahead but at least I could make out some lights ahead of us, a little further down the mountain road. We were coming up on a village of some description. I could make out very little beyond the haze of the lamplight which was coming from the few streets and homes which made up the location, a fuzzy layer of fog was drifting ahead of us as we made our way down. Jane looked on at the light and her eyes started to whip across the foggy surface of the village as we closed the distance. Her breathing was starting to quicken and I could practically taste the escalating fear in her whole body. As we drove, her fear became contagious. What was happening to her? What was going to happen to me?

Crap.

The fog was starting to drift around the car as we moved closer to the village.

"Do you want to get out here?" I asked, hoping that I had managed to hide my own fear at what was going on around us. If this village was where she called home, I could get her out of the car and she would be able to get on with resolving the issue she had been unable or unwilling to resolve in life. That and the ghost wouldn't be in the car anymore.

"I need to get home. Please drop me here." Jane's voice was now a beacon. She was at her destination and knew she had to get out of the car before she went too far. She was pulling at the handle of the door as a way of showing that she really meant what she was saying.

I pulled the car quickly to the side of the road and offered to open the door for her but she was already out into the foggy night, leaving the passenger door wide open. The fog which had been slowly drifting had started to form quite thickly around the car, so much so that Jane had disappeared into it. It was also starting to seep into the car.

I lunged across the passenger seat as fast as I could and heaved the door shut. I didn't know why but I knew that I had to get away from this point on the road and get to my parents house as fast as possible. Aside from the chill which had been snaking around my spine since I had first encountered the lost woman, I felt that I needed to see my own family. If the night's woman in white had been aiming to resolve the disputes of life after death, I think I should give some attention to my own troubles. I didn't want to leave anything I could resolve hanging around.

Pulling out onto the road again, the fog was drifting around my car as thickly as when I had first met Jane. Fingers crossed for no more visitors. Maybe some music would help calm me down. Reaching forward to the radio I blew out a relieved breath that I had resolved to finally clear the air with my family.

'The young woman, named only as Jane, had been involved in a serious car crash whilst traveling home from the airport. She had flown home from Tenerife that day. Her car had left the road at a notorious accident black spot in the hills outside her home village of Huntsforth. Her account of what took place after this terrible event has had local police and residents shocked. We'll let Jane explain in her own words.'

"I crawled back up to the road hoping to flag down a passing car but all I could see was a thick cloud coming down the hillside. It settled on the road and stopped moving, like it had been put there. The car came out almost immediately. The man got out and asked what I was doing out there. I had banged my head so I was feeling a bit fuzzy but he offered to help. He kept asking me where I needed to go, he wanted to know where I was going and kept asking me the same thing, like he couldn't get beyond the need to help. All I could say to him was that I needed to see my mum. When he told me his name was Hugo I knew who he was. He touched my hand in the car and I could feel a buzz of power from him. I let him get me close to home but as soon as I saw the fog forming I knew I had to get out and run away."

The man Hugo that Jane spoke about is Hugo Smith. Hugo's car was found at the same spot that Jane had crashed her car, seven years ago. He had been travelling home to see his family when he left the road and plunged to his death on a foggy night. Locals have reported seeing his car passing through the narrow roads late at night only for it to vanish into a fast forming cloud of fog. Jane's account of her activities have led some to believe that Hugo has been driving the roads after his death in an attempt to save another from the same fate that befell him. Others have dismissed the account from Jane as being the ranting's of a trauma victim who had suffered serious head injuries but people in Huntsforth have reported that Hugo and his car haven't been seen since that night a week ago.

The whole valley has started to speculate that maybe Hugo is finally at peace. Jane herself is certain of what she saw and has said that she wants to contact the family of her spectral Samaritan to thank them for the help their son gave to her.

"I want them to know that Hugo helped me when I was in need. They have to know that he was a good man."

If you or any of your family have any further sightings of the ghostly driver please contact the station.

Origin of the Species

"I don't know."

"Well neither do I."

"None of us do."

Grumbles of noise flickered around the gathered group and they all continued to stare, ponder and worry.

"You guys gave all the same information to everyone, yes? No-one could have missed anything?"

"All of them got the same information, but it would appear that... um... it may be being interpreted in different ways."

A nervous laugh accompanied the last comment. There wasn't much by way of response save for continued worry.

Not good.

"Fine, run me through everything up to this point so we can see exactly what's been going on. We've all spent far too long dealing with this for it to go sour now."

That comment brought a very strong rumbling of agreement from the gathered group, each starting to shuffle together paperwork and charts and readouts of various shapes, colours and even smells.

In a short time, the gathering around the bright table of information had swelled as more and more bodies jostled and bumped to see what was happening on the screen before them. Eventually there was a voice to calm the rabble.

"Everyone gathered. We need to review all of the information we have at hand to try to reach some understanding on the situation we have down there."

More agreeing rumbles.

"So, who wants to go first?"

No-one moved.

"Come on, Base-work, you guys are up."

Nervous movement and a rather portly character was practically pushed from the crowd. Shuffling papers, the talk began.

"All of our work has been maintained in line exactly with what had been expected. We have seen a great push to remove different matters from the base-work over time but so far there have been no incidents of note to call out. Solid as always from our team." Another nervous laugh.

"Solid and boring. Good old Base-work," came whispering through the crowd.

The base-work delegate hurriedly melted back into the group.

"Fine. Solution. What ya got?"

The next speaker lurched forward.

"All Solution has been run in the way we had planned. There is currently a watch out on the balance being maintained but the factors affecting all levels of solution are coming from within." A brisk nod towards the screen and all the other gazes in the darkened room turned to land on the screen table. The image showed an overview of what was being said by the voice of Solution.

Some people nodded and others just looked on. There were a couple who didn't seem to be looking at anything.

"Why is Solution being undermined by the actions of the subjects? What gave them the ideas to do what they're doing?"

"They are taking from base-work as well," chimed the original voice, this time from way in the back of the crowd.

"Thank you base-work, yes I do remember you saying."

Another, more high pitched and irate voice chimed in from the opposite side of the room, again from the back of the gathered bodies.

"There have a great many negative impacts for Bubble – all brought on by the output of one of Populous' groups."

"Thank you Bubble. Is this true Populous? Is your team and its efforts having a negative impact on the work of any of the other groups?"

Silence followed as all the combined attention fell on the group of assembled bodies from Populous. For an eternal second – there was no voice raised in answer and the tension continued to grow.

"Looking at the activities of one of our groups, there has been a great deal of bleed over into other departments work but this has only taken place very recently. Up to this point they have been performing in an accelerated fashion and have been outperforming every other group down there. The recent activities have come as a mystery to us all."

Silence was restored, every gaze still locked on the Populous team.

"Can you explain why they have gone from being the shining jewel in what you're doing to being the one thing that's making everything worse for everyone else? There are more than just your projects running down there and we will not stand by and see everyone else have their efforts attacked just because you didn't act."

Attention still on Populous.

"It was only supposed to give them a little nudge." This time the new voice was tiny and dribbled away almost before the end of the sentence. The head of Populous turned and matched the gazes of everyone else in the room.

"What?"

The little voice was summoned forward and spoke again.

"They were the ones that were showing the greatest promise after we had to re-boot after the previous leaders had slowed down to such a degree, what with the low intelligence. The Populous team were under a great deal of pressure to deliver so after I spoke with my family I decided to make a few tiny adjustments."

"You did what!? Your family? What exactly did you do?" Silence hung over the gathered crowd like a heavy blanket, and by the looks being fired at the Populous delegate who had just spoken, that blanket had a fart underneath it.

"I upgraded the information we gave them in certain aspects. Just a tweak really, hehehehehe."

More silence. Definitely no laughter to join the feeble offering.

This time the question was much more powerful. Slower. More menacing.

"What did you upgrade?" The words were deliberately spoken and there was no missing the anger behind them.

Gulp.

"After the re-boot I thought that we couldn't risk having them stagnate in the same way so I upgraded their curiosity and problem solving so they would move faster but I've been feeling very close to them all so I tried to give them an understanding of what I've done for them so they would appreciate me. I'm working really hard on this and no-one here sees what I do." The comment ended with a little harrumpf.

"YOU DID WHAT?!"

Somehow, the silence got thicker.

"Populous were blamed for the last failure. We all know that everyone was talking about us behind our backs. All I did was try to make sure we had something positive come out of our work."

"Positive?" The leader of Populous was speaking again.

"All these issues we've been monitoring have been down to you?"

Silence again.

"You've mangled the results. Looking at the data now I can clearly see the results of your handy work. The unexplained split we've been monitoring has come from you. This group have advanced because of you, you idiot. Some of them have been working things out at a remarkable rate, controlling everything around them but you've made them uncontrolled over-reachers. They don't know when to stop. Their actions have impinged on the others,

Bubble, Base-Work, Solution, even us. You should see what they've been doing to other sub-projects. They also seem obsessed in coming up here, like they have exhausted all the problems down there. As for this other lot. Your weird desire to make friends has given them all a skewed view of what they are. There are loads of different pods claiming knowledge of you but they all think that they're the ones with the real deal. They're killing each other because of you and the mis-guided idea that you are somehow in charge of everything. How any of them could believe just a single mind put this together is beyond comprehension but you've somehow managed to give them that. And to top it all off, it seems that you have to be one or the other. If the first group thought more like the second group you could slow them down a bit and if the second group thought more like the first group they'd maybe question the idiocy of you and work out things for themselves – like they were supposed to do, just not this fast."

Even more silence.

The booming first voice echoed out over the gathered masses and brought every shred of attention in the room together.

"We can't maintain these conditions, can we?"

"No sir." The leader of Populous was not happy.

Ripples of *"Populous again,"* could be heard whisping about on the ether.

"There really is only one option open to us now isn't there? Re-boot again."

"But sir…"

"I'm not interested Populous. We are all going to have to start again because your team have hashed up everything again. What makes it worse is the fact that the results had started so well but as we all know, you can't fudge figures."

Populous gave disgruntled silence while everyone else stared angrily at them.

"Populous, please re-boot the system so we can…"

A flash of startlingly bright light flashed out from the screens on the table before all assembled.

"Now what have you done Populous?" This time there was just a sigh behind the words. Typical Populous.

Lots of hurried shuffling of paper, pressing of buttons and frowning at screens until there was a collected gasp from every voice in the room.

"They've re-booted themselves sir," said a very prim voice at the nearest edge of the table, but with shocked anger woven through it.

"Populous' meddling re-booted it and have wiped out everything Bubble have done."

"And loads of Solution. Look at the mess."

"Base-work have taken a hit too you know." Shuffle, press, shuffle "but by the looks of things we can be up and running again soon."

"Well they've ruined the rest of our projects too you know." Populous was indignant now. All the hard work, undone by one meddler.

"QUIET!" Shouted the chair of the meeting.

"Populous. Let this be a lesson to you all but, Populous, I want you to listen closest. If any of you attempt to work around the limits of this set up again then I will terminate your involvement in the project completely. We are doing our best to build something of merit here and all you seem to be trying to do is win petty battles amongst yourselves."

Even more silence. The Populous team all kept their gazes down at the floor.

"Now, moving on. Base-work, are you able to continue as is?"

"Yes sir."

"Bubble?"

"Possibly, but we've got to run a wipe of most of what we've got left."

"Good enough. Solution?"

"Much like Bubble but doable, sir."

"Good. I suggest we use this event as a learning tool and make certain that this never happens again. From anyone."

A collected round of hushed agreements followed.

"So Populous. What are you going to use now?"

Uncomfortable shifting of weight, everyone waiting on the answer.

"Um, fish sir. I think that we will be in a stronger position to work with Solution if our main project links in with them."

"Good idea. So we've all learned that Dinosaurs and now Humans have proved to be a very poor showing. Let's see if working together with another department can improve what you do."

"What if there are any remnants from the last round of Populous?"

"Just leave them. What's the worse they could do?"

About the Author

Owen is a fan of all forms of storytelling and enjoys books, film and TV, as long as there's something compelling going on. He's worked in different roles over the years, but has always had the spark of creativity lurking in the back of his mind. A Welsh rugby supporter, he lives in South Wales with his wife Joanne and they are protected by their new guardian cat, Sausage. Baggins is no longer with us, but Sausage is the cat to carry on his work.

Visit Owen Elgie on [Facebook](), [Twitter](), and [Wordpress]().